Playing electric bass from chord symbols is absolutely necessary for the musician desiring to play in amateur and professional bands and orchestras. Roger Filiberto has presented a detailed and easily understandable method for reading chord symbols. I recommend this book for every electric bass player from beginner to professional.

Mel Bay

1 2 3 4 5 6 7 8 9 0

© COPYRIGHT 1978 BY MEL BAY PUBLICATIONS, INC., PACIFIC, MO.
INTERNATIONAL COPYRIGHT SECURED • ALL RIGHTS RESERVED • PRINTED IN U.S.A.

AUTHOR'S NOTE

This method will make it possible for the bassist to play from chord symbols and most importantly will give the performer the opportunity to learn "chord spelling" and acquire a good foundation in chord construction.

All of the patterns are moveable and may be played chromatically up or down the fingerboard thus enabling the bassist to play in various keys.

For maximum results, follow the musical notation—but carefully observe the fingering and the positions of the patterns in the tablature.

THE TABLATURE

```
Strings  1 _____5_____
         2 _____5_____2____5_____
         3 _____2____5_____3_____
         4 __3_____
```

Each space designates a string (bottom to top — 4-3-2-1)

The numbers in the spaces indicate the fret positions of the notes being played.

In the musical notation the numbers beside the notes indicate the fingers.

*ENHARMONIC CHART

C♯ is D♭   G♯ is A♭
D♯ is E♭   A♯ is B♭
E♯ is F   B♯ is C
F♯ is G♭

It is important that you study and learn each note and its enharmonic. For example A♯ is rarely shown as such. In the event you should come across an A♯ chord of any description, major, minor, 7th etc., simply refer to the B♭ chord in the same category. It is enharmonically the same. The D♯ chord is rare. Refer to its enharmonic, which is E♭. B♯ is extremely rare. Refer to C chord. Still another example is the E♯ chord. Refer to its enharmonic "F."

*(Note: Enharmonic means change of letter but not change of pitch)

CONTENTS

C

- C Major 7
- C Minor 15
- C Diminished 29
- C Augmented 29
- C Seventh 22
- C Minor Seventh 29
- C Seventh Aug. Fifth 29
- C Seventh Flat Fifth 29
- C Major Seventh 29
- C Min-Maj Seventh 29
- C Minor Seventh ♭5th 29
- C7 Suspended 4th 29
- C Sixth 29
- C Minor Sixth 29
- C Ninth 29
- C Minor Ninth 29
- C Major Ninth 29
- C9 #5th 29
- C9 ♭5th 29
- C7 ♭9 29
- C7 #9 29
- C6 add 9th 29
- C Eleventh 29
- C Aug. Eleventh 29
- C Thirteenth 29
- C 13−9 29
- C 13−9−5 29

D♭ Or C#

- D♭ Major 7
- D♭ Minor 15
- D♭ Diminished 30
- D♭ Augmented 30
- D♭ Seventh 23
- D♭ Minor Seventh 30
- D♭ Seventh Aug. Fifth 30
- D♭ Seventh Flat Fifth 30
- D♭ Major Seventh 30
- D♭ Min-Maj Seventh 30
- D♭ Minor Seventh ♭5th 30
- D♭7 Suspended 4th 30
- D♭ Sixth 30
- D♭ Minor Sixth 30
- D♭ Ninth 30
- D♭ Minor Ninth 30
- D♭ Major Ninth 30
- D♭9 #5th 30
- D♭9 ♭5th 30
- D♭7 ♭9 30
- D♭7 #9 30
- D♭ 6 Add 9th 30
- D♭ Eleventh 30
- D♭ Aug. Eleventh 30
- D♭ Thirteenth 30
- D♭ 13−9 30
- D♭ 13−9−5 30

D

- D Major 8
- D Minor 16
- D Diminished 31
- D Augmented 31
- D Seventh 23
- D Minor Seventh 31
- D Seventh Aug. Fifth 31
- D Seventh Flat Fifth 31
- D Major Seventh 31
- D Min-Maj Seventh 31
- D Minor Seventh ♭5th 31
- D7 Suspended 4th 31
- D Sixth 31
- D Minor Sixth 31
- D Ninth 31
- D Minor Ninth 31
- D Major Ninth 31
- D9 #5th 31
- D9 ♭5th 31
- D7 ♭9 31
- D7 #9 31
- D 6 add 9th 31
- D Eleventh 31
- D Aug. Eleventh 31
- D Thirteenth 31
- D 13−9 31
- D 13−9−5 31

E♭ or D#

- E♭ Major 9
- E♭ Minor 17
- E♭ Diminished 32
- E♭ Augmented 32
- E♭ Seventh 24
- E♭ Minor Seventh 32
- E♭ Seventh Aug. Fifth 32
- E♭ Seventh Flat Fifth 32
- E♭ Major Seventh 32
- E♭ Min-Maj Seventh 32
- E♭ Minor Seventh ♭5th 32
- E♭7 Suspended 4th 32
- E♭ Sixth 32
- E♭ Minor Sixth 32
- E♭ Ninth 32
- E♭ Minor Ninth 32
- E♭ Major Ninth 32
- E♭9 #5th 32
- E♭9 ♭5th 32
- E♭7 ♭9 32
- E♭7 #9 32
- E♭6 add 9th 32
- E♭ Eleventh 32
- E♭ Aug. Eleventh 32
- E♭ Thirteenth 32
- E♭ 13−9 32
- E♭ 13−9−5 32

E

- E Major 10
- E Minor 17
- E Diminished 33
- E Augmented 33
- E Seventh 24
- E Minor Seventh 33
- E Seventh Aug. Fifth 33
- E Seventh Flat Fifth 33
- E Major Seventh 33
- E Min-Maj Seventh 33
- E Minor Seventh ♭5th 33
- E7 Suspended 4th 33
- E Sixth 33
- E Minor Sixth 33
- E Ninth 33
- E Minor Ninth 33
- E Major Ninth 33
- E9 #5th 33
- E9 ♭5th 33
- E7 ♭9 33
- E7 #9 33
- E 6 add 9 33
- E Eleventh 33
- E Aug. Eleventh 33
- E Thirteenth 33
- E 13−9 33
- E 13−9−5 33

F Or E#

- F Major 11
- F Minor 18
- F Diminished 34
- F Augmented 34
- F Seventh 24
- F Minor Seventh 34
- F Seventh Aug. Fifth 34
- F Seventh Flat Fifth 34
- F Major Seventh 34
- F Min-Maj Seventh 34
- F Minor Seventh ♭5th 34
- F7 Suspended 4th 34
- F Sixth 34
- F Minor Sixth 34
- F Ninth 34
- F Minor Ninth 34
- F Major Ninth 34
- F9 #5th 34
- F9 ♭5th 34
- F7 ♭9 34
- F7 #9 34
- F 6 add 9 34
- F Eleventh 34
- F Aug. Eleventh 34
- F Thirteenth 34
- F 13−9 34
- F 13−9−5 34

G♭ Or F#

Chord	Page
G♭ Major	12
G♭ Minor	18
G♭ Diminished	35
G♭ Augmented	35
G♭ Seventh	25
G♭ Minor Seventh	35
G♭ Seventh Aug. Fifth	35
G♭ Seventh Flat Fifth	35
G♭ Major Seventh	35
G♭ Min-Maj Seventh	35
G♭ Minor Seventh ♭5th	35
G♭7 Suspended 4th	35
G♭ Sixth	35
G♭ Minor Sixth	35
G♭ Ninth	35
G♭ Minor Ninth	35
G♭ Major Ninth	35
G♭9 #5th	35
G♭9 ♭5th	35
G♭7 ♭9	35
G♭7 #9	35
G♭ 6 add 9	35
G♭ Eleventh	35
G♭ Aug. Eleventh	35
G♭ Thirteenth	35
G♭ 13 −9	35
G♭ 13 −9 −5	35

G

Chord	Page
G Major	12
G Minor	19
G Diminished	36
G Augmented	36
G Seventh	26
G Minor Seventh	36
G Seventh Aug. Fifth	36
G Seventh Flat Fifth	36
G Major Seventh	36
G Min-Maj Seventh	36
G Minor Seventh ♭5th	36
G7 Suspended 4th	36
G Sixth	36
G Minor Sixth	36
G Ninth	36
G Minor Ninth	36
G Major Ninth	36
G9 #5th	36
G9 ♭5th	36
G7 ♭9	36
G7 #9	36
G 6 add 9	36
G Eleventh	36
G Aug. Eleventh	36
G Thirteenth	36
G 13 −9	36
G 13 −9 −5	36

A♭ Or G#

Chord	Page
A♭ Major	13
A♭ Minor	19-20
A♭ Diminished	37
A♭ Augmented	37
A♭ Seventh	26-27
A♭ Minor Seventh	37
A♭ Seventh Aug. Fifth	37
A♭ Seventh Flat Fifth	37
A♭ Major Seventh	37
A♭ Min-Maj Seventh	37
A♭ Minor Seventh ♭5th	37
A♭7 Suspended 4th	37
A♭ Sixth	37
A♭ Minor Sixth	37
A♭ Ninth	37
A♭ Minor Ninth	37
A♭ Major Ninth	37
A♭9 #5th	37
A♭9 ♭5th	37
A♭7 ♭9	37
A♭7 #9	37
A♭ 6 add 9	37
A♭ Eleventh	37
A♭ Aug. Eleventh	37
A♭ Thirteenth	37
A♭ 13 −9	37
A♭ 13 −9 −5	37

A

Chord	Page
A Major	13
A Minor	20
A Diminished	38
A Augmented	38
A Seventh	27
A Minor Seventh	38
A Seventh Aug. Fifth	38
A Seventh Flat Fifth	38
A Major Seventh	38
A Min-Maj Seventh	38
A Minor Seventh ♭5th	38
A7 Suspended 4th	38
A Sixth	38
A Minor Sixth	38
A Ninth	38
A Minor Ninth	38
A Major Ninth	38
A9 #5th	38
A9 ♭5th	38
A7 ♭9	38
A7 #9	38
A 6 add 9	38
A Eleventh	38
A Aug. Eleventh	38
A Thirteenth	38
A 13 −9	38
A 13 −9 −5	38

B♭ Or A#

Chord	Page
B♭ Major	14
B♭ Minor	21
B♭ Diminished	39
B♭ Augmented	39
B♭ Seventh	28
B♭ Minor Seventh	39
B♭ Seventh Aug. Fifth	39
B♭ Seventh Flat Fifth	39
B♭ Major Seventh	39
B♭ Min-Maj Seventh	39
B♭ Minor Seventh ♭5th	39
B♭7 Suspended 4th	39
B♭ Sixth	39
B♭ Minor Sixth	39
B♭ Ninth	39
B♭ Minor Ninth	39
B♭ Major Ninth	39
B♭9 #5th	39
B♭9 ♭5th	39
B♭7 ♭9	39
B♭7 #9	39
B♭ 6 add 9	39
B♭ Eleventh	39
B♭ Aug. Eleventh	39
B♭ Thirteenth	39
B♭ 13 −9	39
B♭ 13 −9 −5	39

B Or C♭

Chord	Page
B Major	14
B Minor	21
B Diminished	40
B Augmented	40
B Seventh	28
B Minor Seventh	40
B Seventh Aug. Fifth	40
B Seventh Flat Fifth	40
B Major Seventh	40
B Min-Maj Seventh	40
B Minor Seventh ♭5th	40
B7 Suspended 4th	40
B Sixth	40
B Minor Sixth	40
B Ninth	40
B Minor Ninth	40
B Major Ninth	40
B9 #5th	40
B9 ♭5th	40
B7 ♭9	40
B7 #9	40
B 6 add 9	40
B Eleventh	40
B Aug. Eleventh	40
B Thirteenth	40
B 13 −9	40
B 13 −9 −5	40

RULES TO OBSERVE

Do not attempt to learn all of the patterns at one time. Stick to one key until you have a fairly good knowledge of it. Memorize the first measures in studies No. 1 and No. 2. We suggest that you start off by learning the C Major, C Minor and C Seventh chords. In this manner you will learn how closely related these three chords are. Notice that the Root and Fifth are the same for each of these chords.

For your first effort try playing the usual "Rock" or "Blues" tunes which, as a rule are usually limited to three changes. As a starter, practice in the Key of C. Your three principal chords are derived from the Scale. These are the Tonic or 1st note of the scale, the Sub Dominant or 4th note of the scale and the Dominant 7th which is the 5th note of the scale. Thus in the Key of C major your principal chords will be C major, F major and G7th. In the Rock or Blues tunes the Sub Dominant can also be played as a Seventh chord. When you have learned these chords fairly well you may then move on to tunes with more changes.

Learn the spelling of the chords. You will find the notes that make up the chords at the top of each page of the Major, Minor and Seventh Chords. The chord spelling for C Major is CEG. For C Minor it is CE♭G, and for C7th it is CEGB♭. We again call your attention to the Root and Fifth which will be the same for all three chords.

Furthermore, the Root and Fifth will be the same for the following chords: Ninths, Major 7th, Minor 7th, Major Sixth, Minor 6th, Major 9, Minor 9, the 9+, Eleventh, the 11+, Thirteenth, the 13 minus 9, and the Six-Nine chord sometimes shown 9 over 6. This will convince you of the importance of the Root and Fifth.

The Root and Flat 5th is the same in the Diminished, the Seventh ♭5, the Ninth ♭5 and the Thirteenth ♭5.

The Root and Sharped Fifth is the same for the Augmented Chords, the Seventh #5 and the Ninth #5. Once again the importance of the Root and Fifth surfaces. It is the back-bone of all Bass parts and is the key to becoming an expert bassist. Admittedly it is the foundation in learning chord spelling. When in doubt as to what to play you'll never go wrong using the Root and Fifth always keeping in mind that in all diminished and flat 5th chords the combination will be the Root and Flat 5, and in all augmented and sharp 5th chords it will be the Root and sharped 5th.

All of the suggested fingering is practical. But it is also OPTIONAL. If you have a better idea USE IT! Initiative is encouraged.

All of the patterns are MOVEABLE...(no open strings). This makes it very easy to transpose. Transposition charts will be found in the G Major and A Major pages.

Instructions in playing the same pattern in a different position will be found in the C Minor and F Minor pages, foot-notes to studies No. 2 and No. 3. A Fine example of the same pattern in two different positions will be found in Study No. 3, the F Minor page. More on this subject will be found in study No. 3, the C Seventh page.

Of great importance to the Bassist is the changing of the Rhythmic figures in order to create variety in "Walk" patterns. This will add "color" to your bass style. See example in study No. 3, the D Minor page.

All No. 1 studies relate to the Root and Fifth combination. All studies No. 2 are single measure patterns. All studies No. 3 are two measure patterns. All studies Number 4 are in 3/4 time. You can use any combination of measures in the No. 2 studies to form patterns of two or more measures if and when needed.

Obviously in chords with five, six and seven notes such as the Ninths with 5 notes, the Elevenths with 6 notes and the Thirteenths with 7 notes we could not maintain a good "Walk" style and use all of the notes of the chord. We therefore used those notes which were most important to the development of a good bass line.

Just as a guitarist makes several inversions of a chord so can the Bassist. Change the sequence of the notes in each pattern where possible and above all "if it sounds good." For example: the C Major chord in study No. 2 (1st measure) is shown in this order. C, C8va, G and E. Invert to play C, E, G and C8va...or C, G, E and C 8va. The notes are the same. Only the order in which they follow changes.

Somewhere in the future it's going to be up to you.

HOW TO USE THIS METHOD
A message to all bassists

How often have you been confronted with this dilemma — there is no bass part available, but nevertheless you are expected to perform. The eight and twelve bar "Rock" and "Blues" tunes with only three or four chord changes are easy to "fake". But what do you do when you are expected to play the more difficult and sophisticated tunes which are "loaded" with numerous chord changes. You are on the well known spot. Perhaps you are one of that rare breed of musicians blessed with an excellent ear. If so, you are one of a small minority. Now, through this method "Play Electric Bass from Chord Symbols" your problems are practically over. No more guessing and probing. The chord symbols to most tunes are readily available. You can find chord symbols on all guitar parts and a great many piano parts, mostly in sheet music. But even if the chord symbols are not available, the guitarist in your group can easily fill you in. If there is no guitarist in your group the pianist or organist can help.

PLAYING THE ELECTRIC BASS FROM CHORD SYMBOLS
The guitar accompaniment

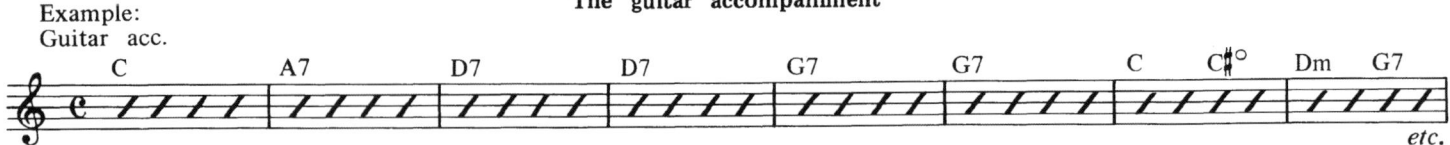

Begin by checking the time signature which is in Common Time, or four beats to the measure. If you are not familiar with guitar parts, each diagonal line represents one beat. This example is in the key of C Major, and begins with a C Major Chord. Refer to the "Contents" pages three and four, find the C Major page and use the first measure in either of the No. 1 or No. 2 studies. You can use any of the Common Time patterns on this page, but our suggestion is to move ahead slowly, limiting yourself to the patterns in the first measures of studies No. 1 or No. 2. Move on to the next measure which is the A7 chord. Once again, refer to the "Contents", look up the A7 page and use the first measure of either one of the studies No. 1 or No. 2. Continue in the same manner until you reach the 7th and 8th measures. You will observe that there are two chord changes of two beats each in both of these measures. The easiest and most effective way to resolve this problem will be to double the root of each of the chord changes. Until you become more familiar with the chord changes we recommend that you use the Root and Fifth or the doubled Root to all chord changes of two beats each. Use a "Walk" style - one bass note for each beat.

Complete your version of a Bass part to the Guitar accompaniment score above. Then compare your version with ours, shown in the two examples below.

The Root and Fifth

*Observe that in the 7th and 8th measures we use the Root only as half notes with two counts each.

In Ex:2 the chord changes are all taken from studies No.2 for the first six measures. Measures seven and eight are taken from study No.1 using the doubled root (Letter name of Chord)

In order to help you through the early stages we recommend the following short cuts. You can substitute the Major Chord for any Seventh, Ninth, Eleventh and Thirteenth chord with the same letter name. You can also substitute the Seventh chord for any Ninth, Eleventh and Thirteenth chord with the same letter name. Ex: Substitute the C Major chord for the C7, C9, C11 and C13. Substitute the C7 chord for the C9, C11 and C13 chords. Remember, this is just a short cut and not to be used permanently, but just in the early stages of learning in order to help you play from chord symbols in the shortest possible time.

Finally, in all measures with two or more chords play the Root of the chord. The Root is the letter name of the chord. The Root of C Major is C...the Root of D7 is D...the Root of C# diminished is C#...the Root of Bb 13 b5 b9 is Bb. These are a few at random examples.

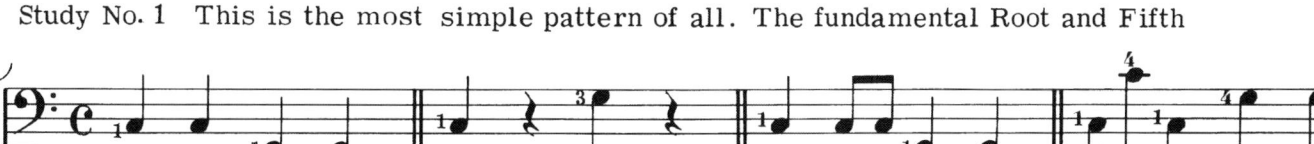

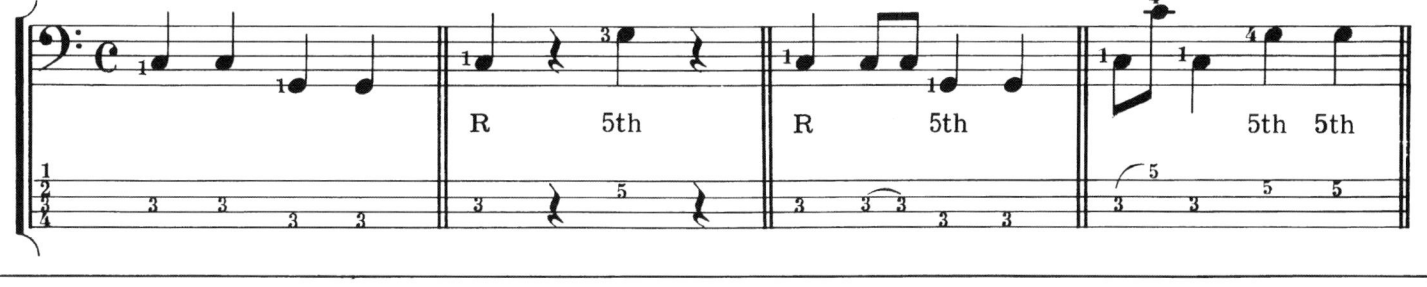

Study No. 1 This is the most simple pattern of all. The fundamental Root and Fifth

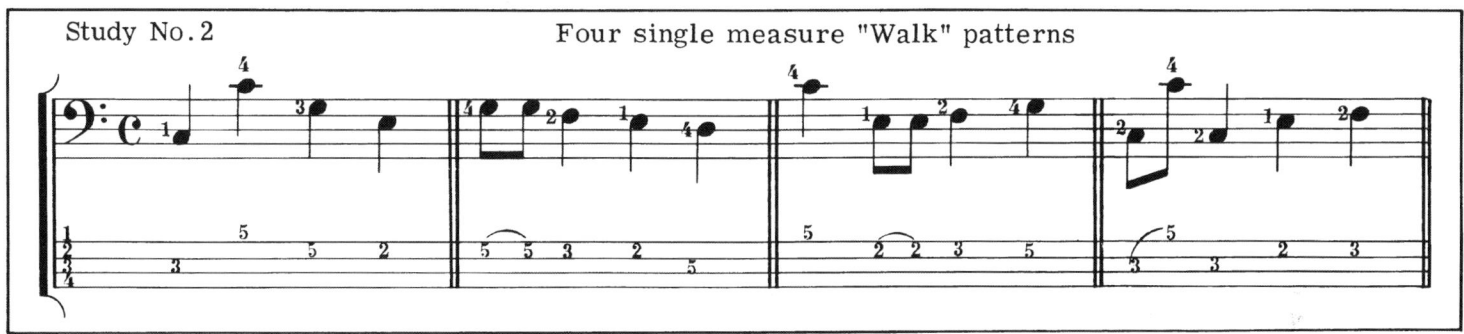

Study No. 2   Four single measure "Walk" patterns

Study No. 3 Two "Walk" patterns of two measures each. Best when used as such. May be repeated to form four measure pattern.

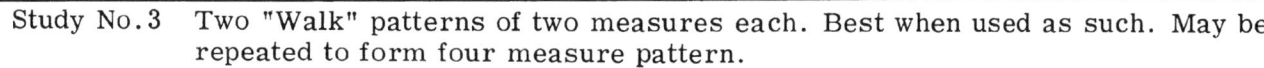

An assortment of 3/4 time patterns

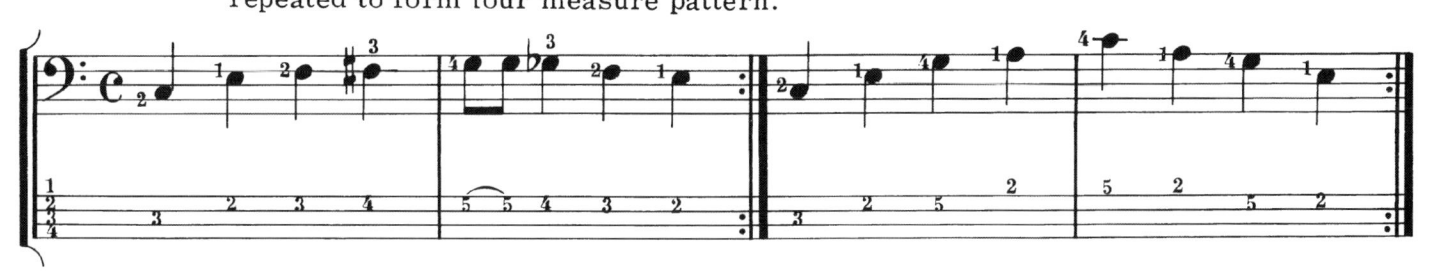

Study No. 4

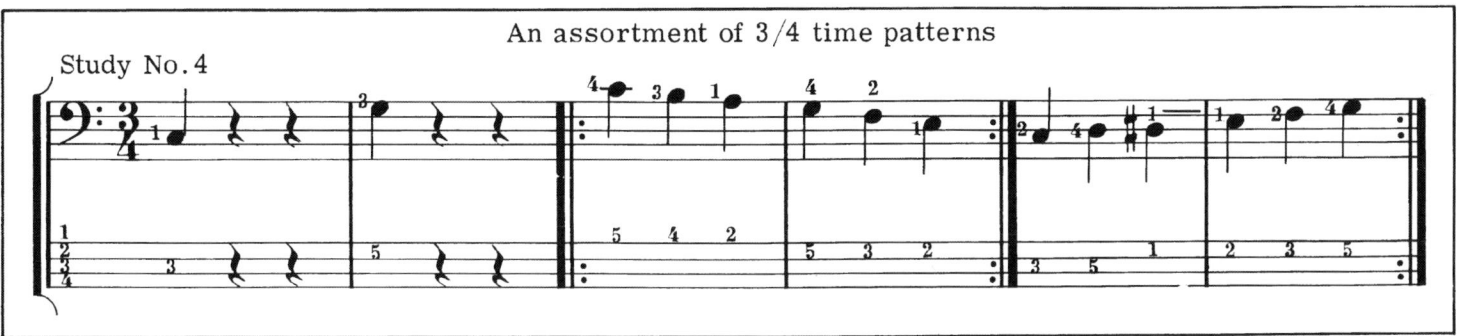

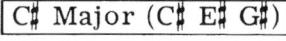

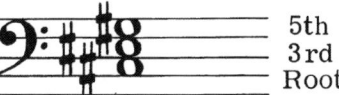

The C♯ Major chord does not occur too often. Since all of the C Major patterns are moveable, (no open strings) you may use any of the above C Major patterns, refer to the tablature and <u>raise</u> each note one fret.

EXAMPLE

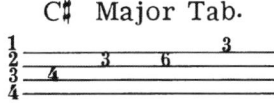

D Major (D F# A) 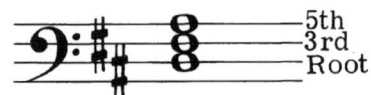 SYMBOL (D)

Study No. 1 — The Root and Fifth
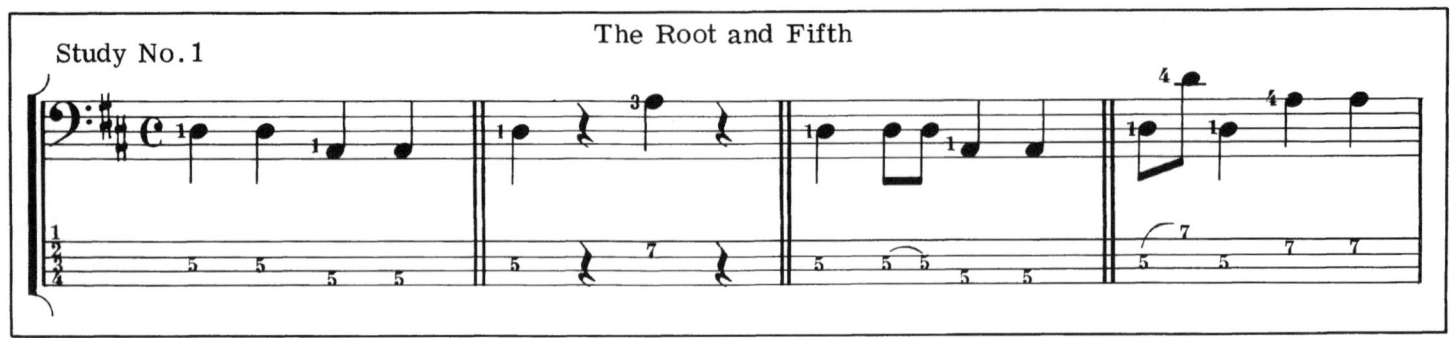

Study No. 2 — Four single measures of "Walk" patterns.
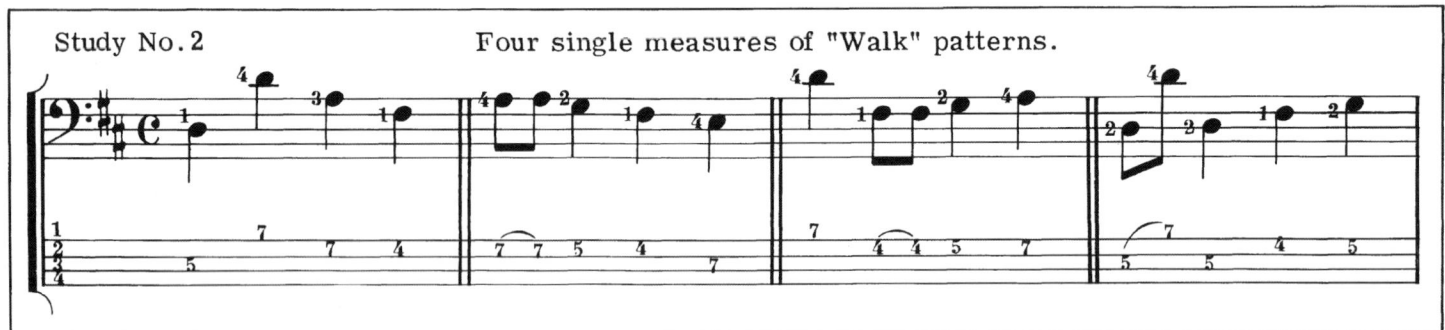

Study No. 3 — Two "Walk" patterns of two measures each.
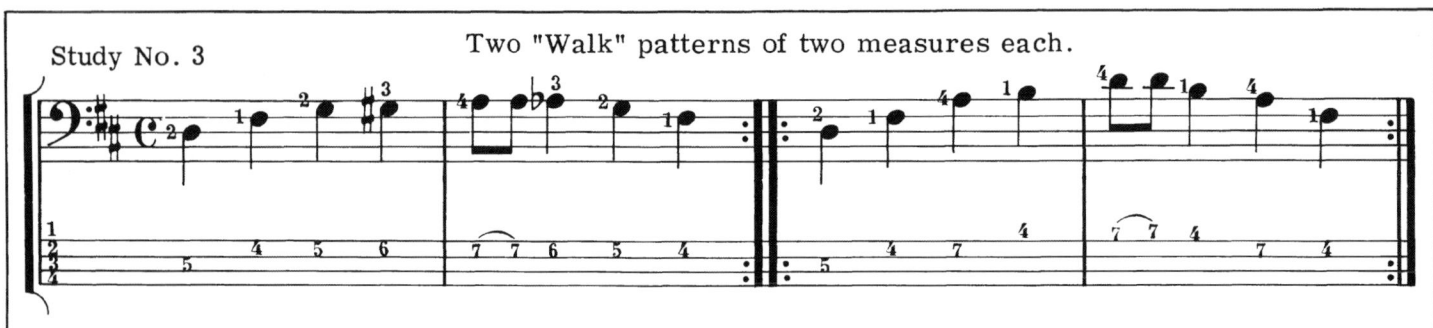

Study No. 4 — 3/4 time patterns
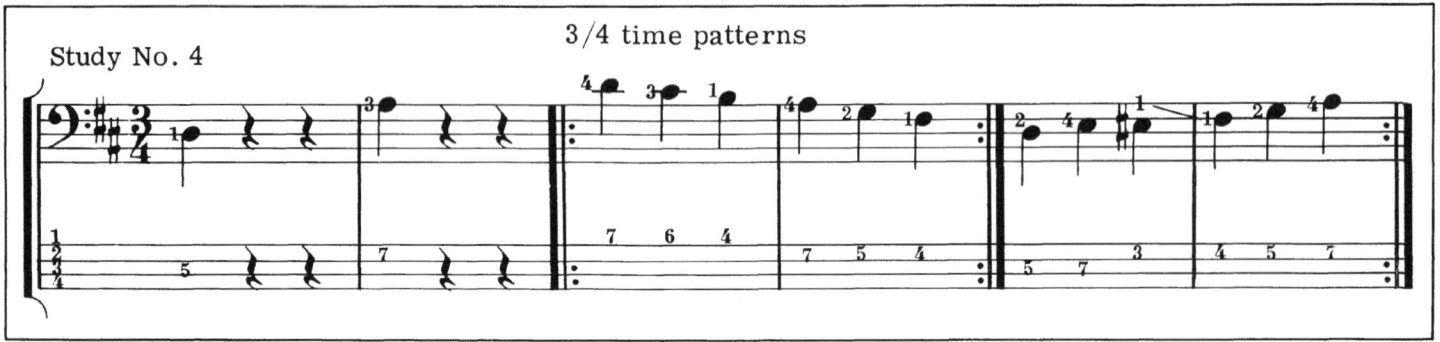

Db Major (Db F Ab)
Bb Eb Ab Db Gb
 SYMBOL (Db)

Db Major and C# Major are the same chord. Since all of the D Major patterns are moveable, (no open strings) you may use any of the above D Major patterns, refer to the tablature and <u>lower</u> each note one fret.

EXAMPLE

D Major Tab. 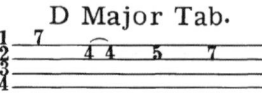   Db Major Tab.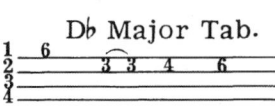

8

Eb Major. (Eb G Bb)

SYMBOL (Eb)

Study No. 1 — The Root and Fifth

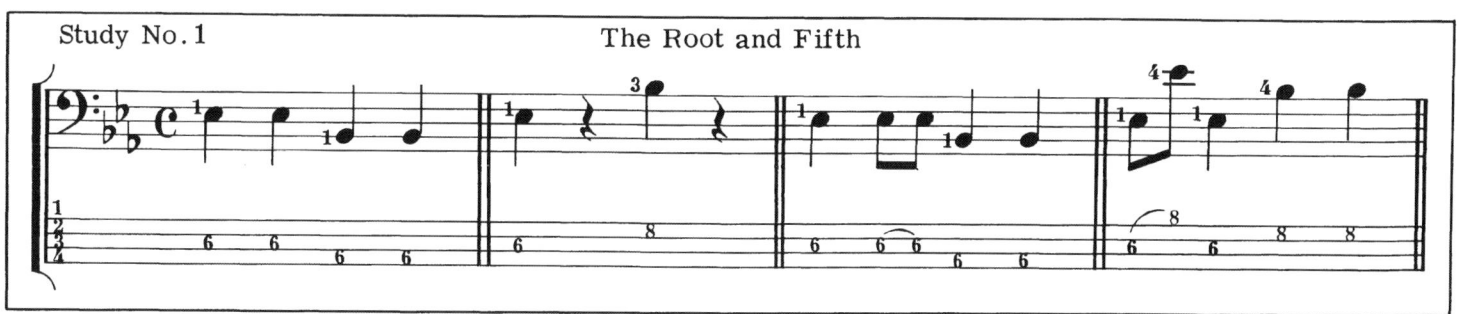

* REMINDER ! All suggested fingering is optional. If you believe that you can come up with a better fingering, USE IT! Originality and inventiveness is encouraged.

Study No. 2 — Four single measures of "Walk" patterns.

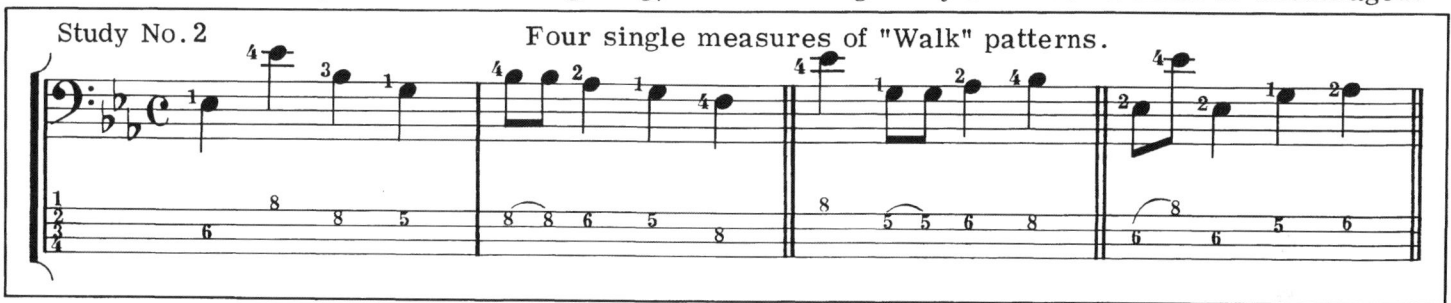

Study No. 3 — Two "Walk" patterns of two measures each.

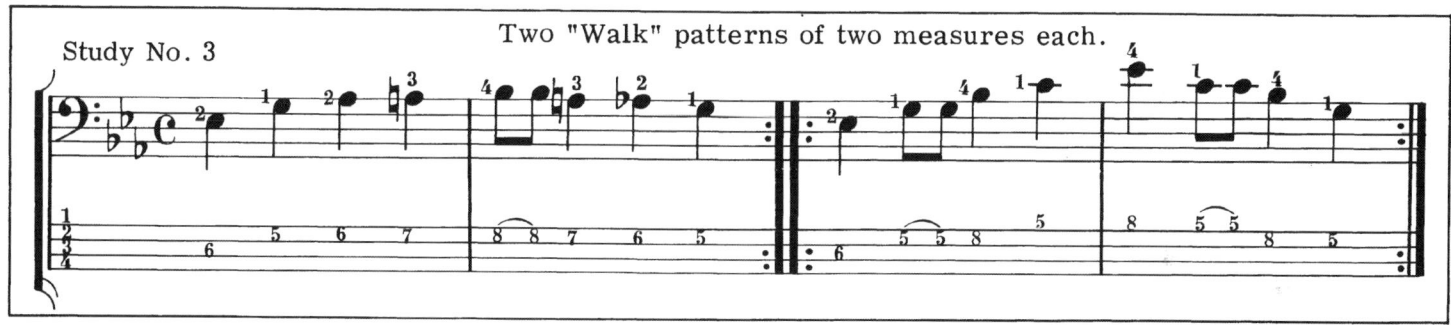

Study No. 4 — 3/4 time patterns

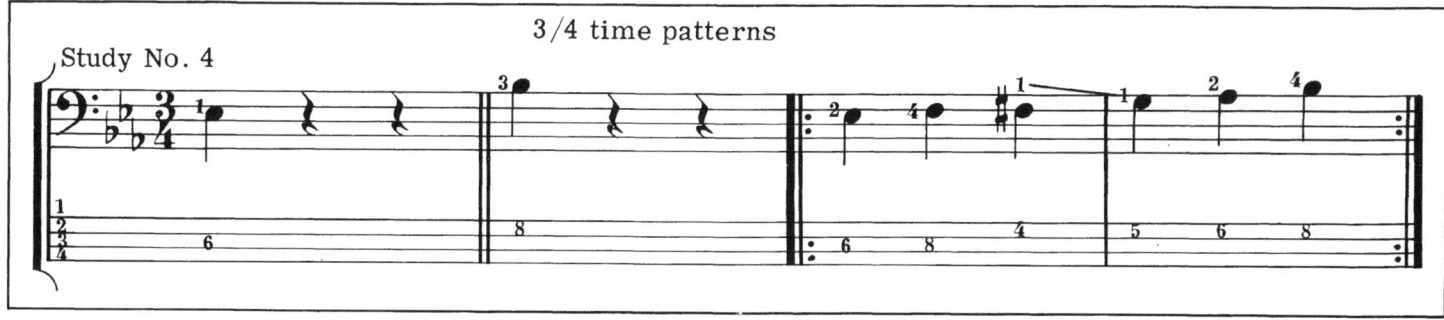

Study No. 5 — Two examples of "pop" Bass styles

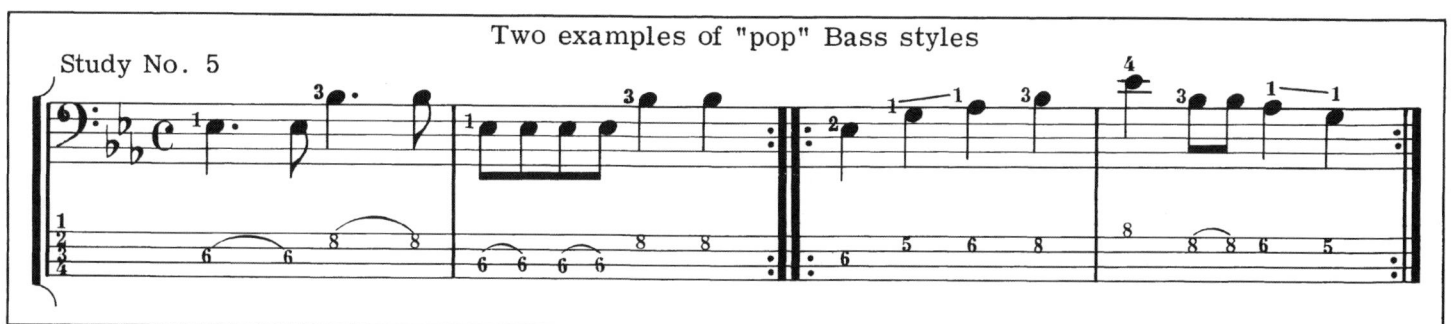

TO IMPROVE YOUR TECHNIC AND KNOWLEDGE OF POSITIONS SEE THE
MEL BAY PUBLICATION "ELECTRIC BASS POSITION STUDIES."

E Major (E G# B) 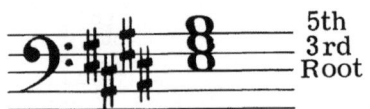 SYMBOL (E)

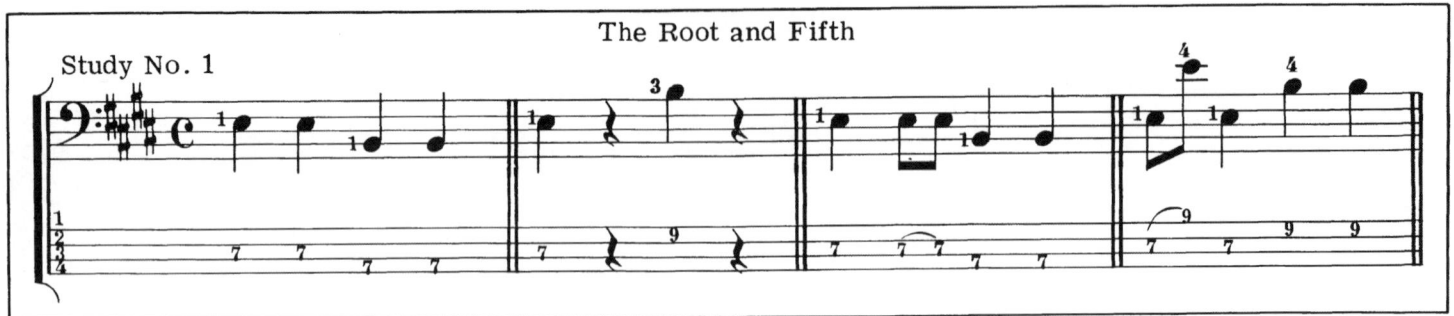

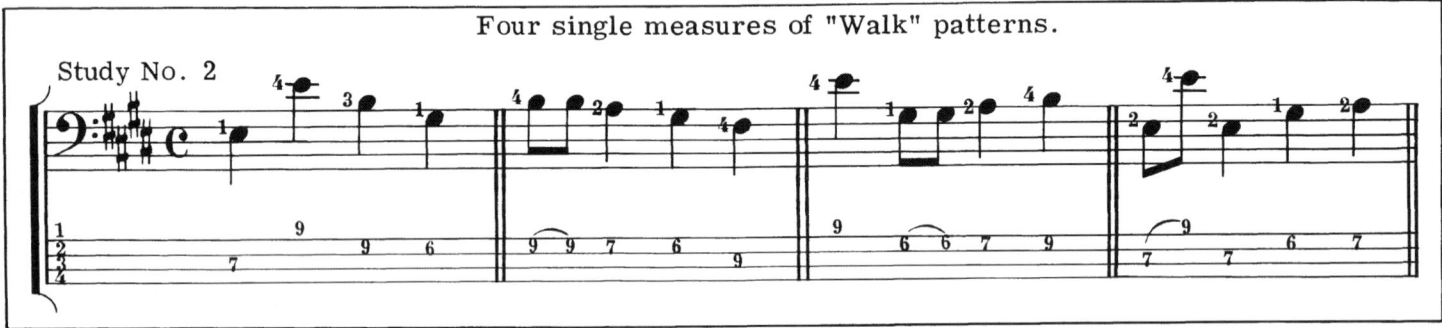

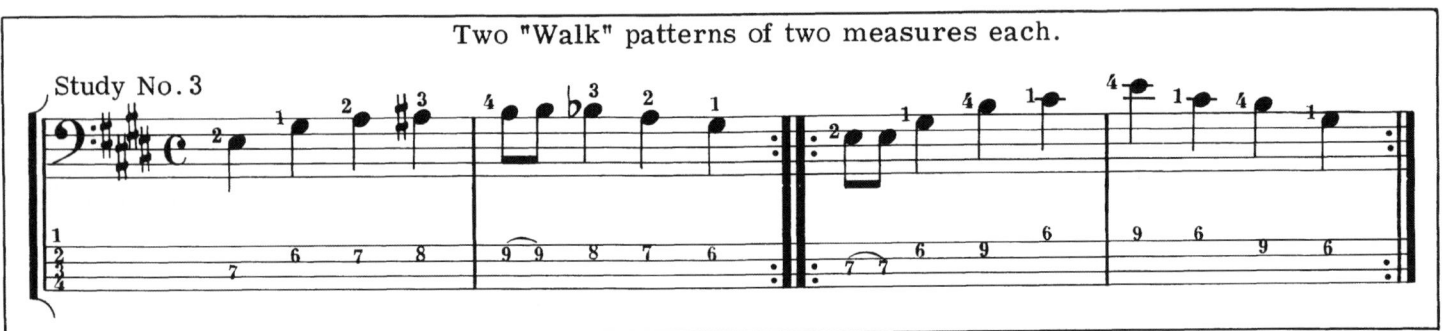

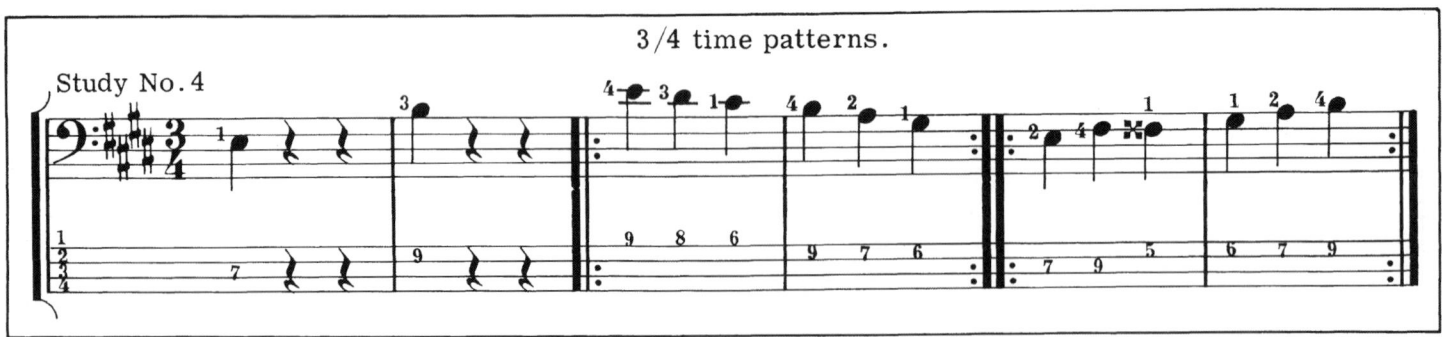

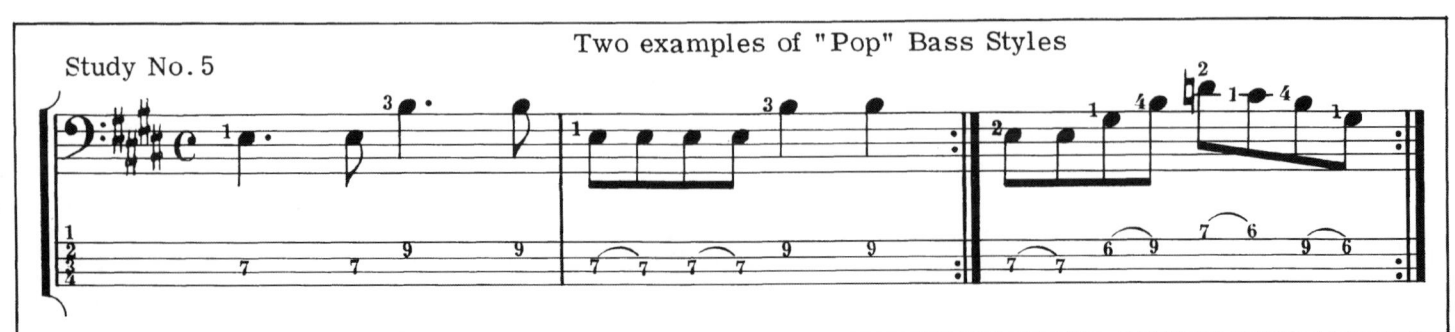

F Major (F A C) 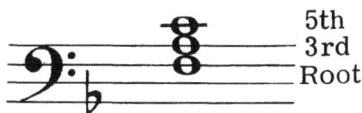 5th / 3rd / Root SYMBOL (F)

Study No. 1 — The Root and Fifth
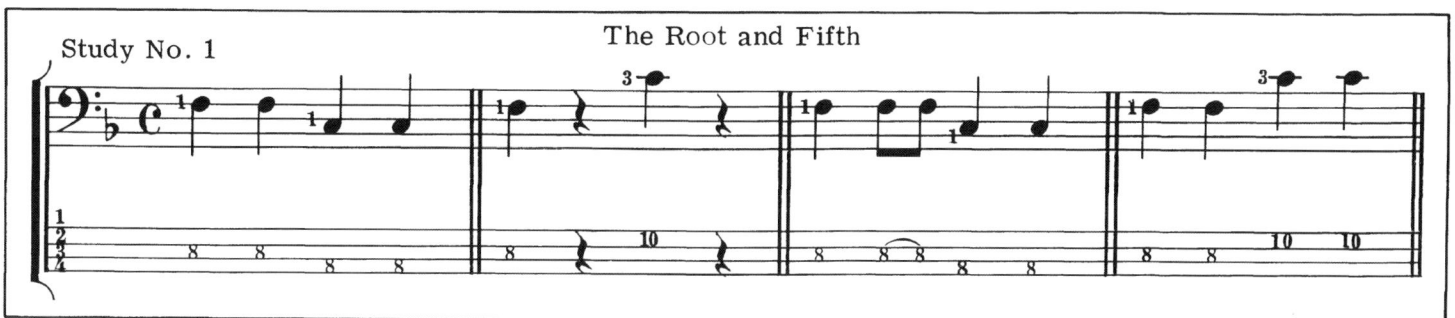

Study No. 2 — Four single measures of "Walk" patterns
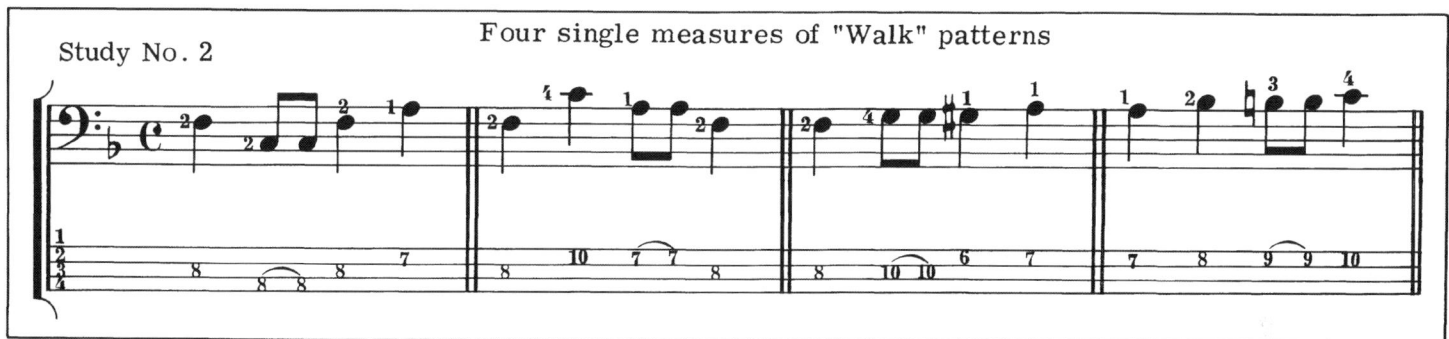

Study No. 3 — Two "Walk" patterns of two measures each

Study No. 4 — An assortment of 3/4 time patterns
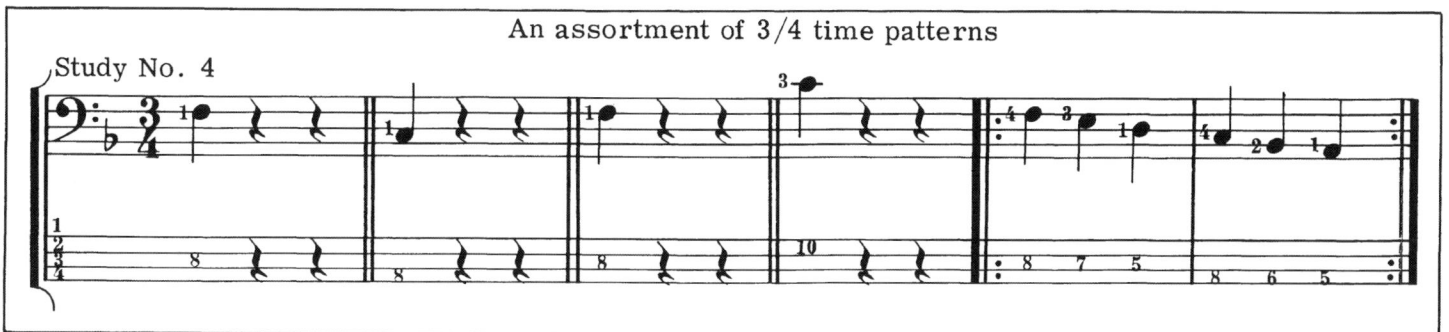

How to play in different keys

All patterns in this book are moveable (no open strings). You can change to another key by simply raising or lowering the pattern wherever practical. This rule applies to ALL patterns. Keep in mind that any study in which the 1st fret is used can only be RAISED. Practice all pages in as many keys as possible.
This will increase your knowledge of the instrument and make you a better Bassist.

G Major (G B D)   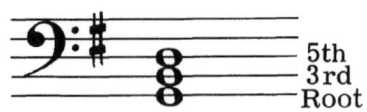   SYMBOL (G)

Study No. 1 — The Root and Fifth

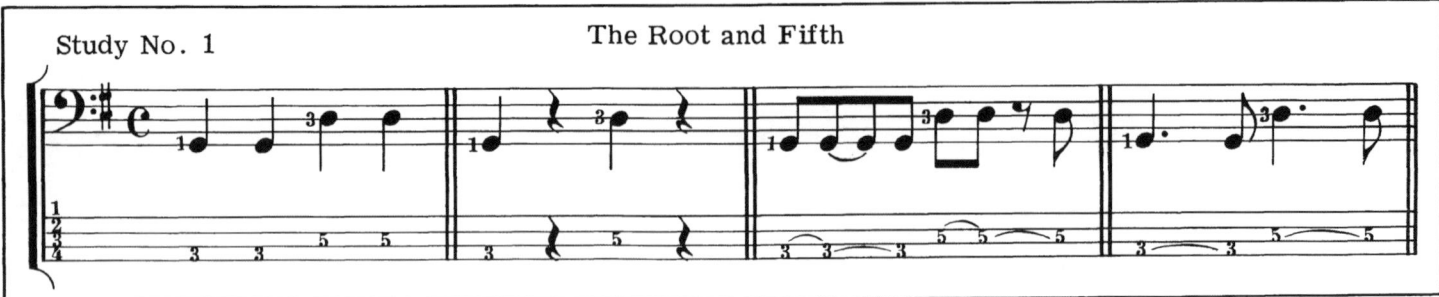

Practice transposition. The G chord is easy to transpose. The most simple approach, the least complicated pattern is that which begins on the third fret, with the G note, or root. Begin this pattern at the fifth fret and you will play the A major chord. Begin on the eighth fret and you will play the C major chord. Try it! Discover the simplicity of transposing the moveable patterns.

Study No. 2 — Four single measures of "Walk" and "Rock" patterns

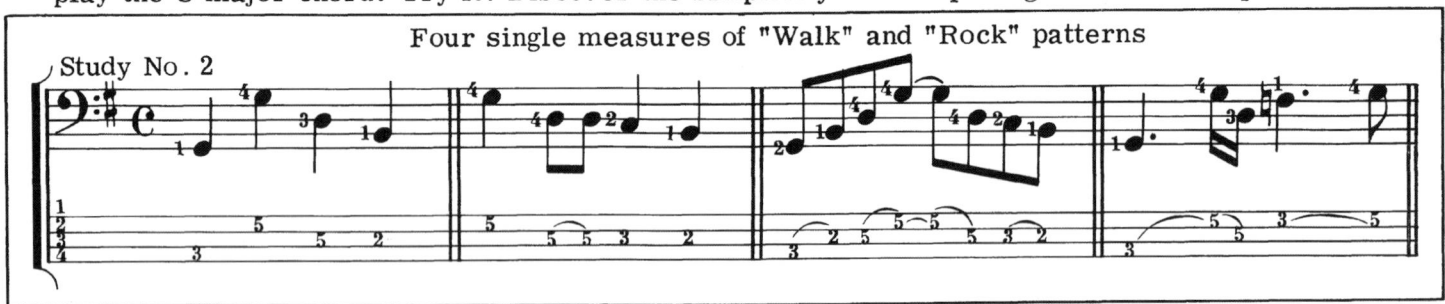

Study No. 3 — Two patterns of two measures each

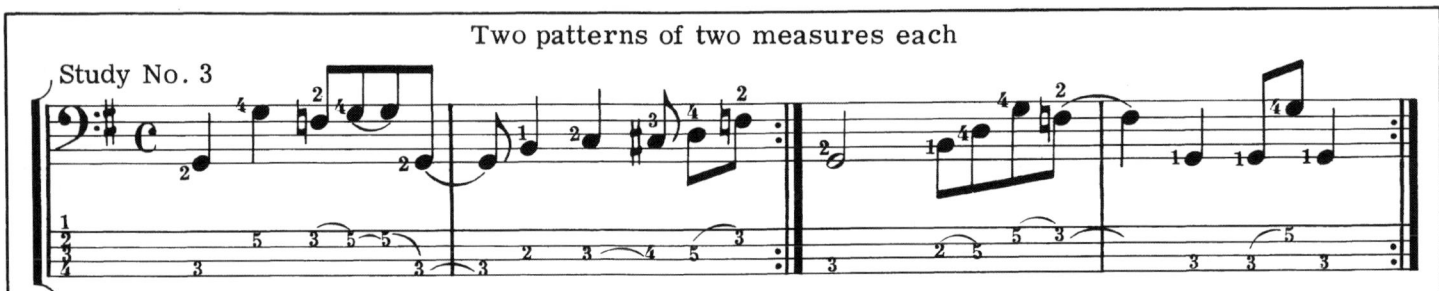

Now that you have tried transposing the G chord pattern to the A major chord, 5th fret and the C Major chord, 8th fret, practise all chords listed below.

FRET	3	4	5	6	7	8	9	10	11	12
CHORD	G	A♭	A	B♭	B	C	D♭	D	E♭	E

Study No. 4 — Various 3/4 time patterns

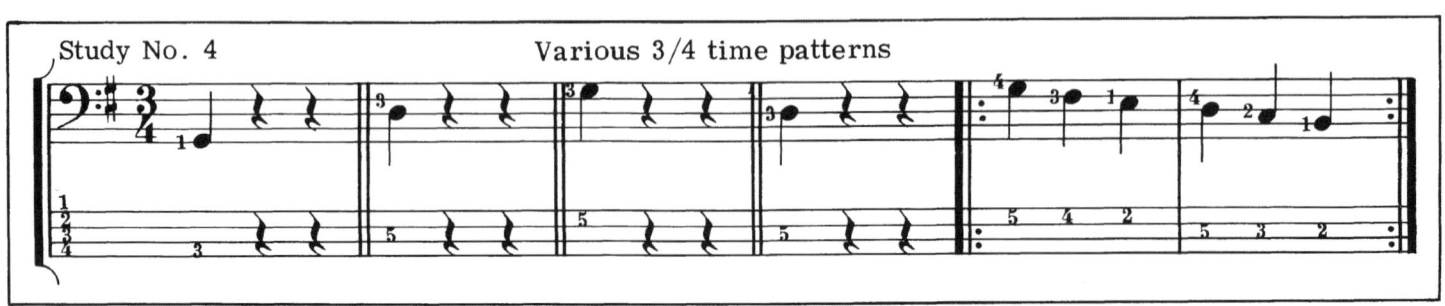

G♭ Major (G♭ B♭ D♭)
SYMBOL (G♭) 6 flats
B♭ E♭ A♭ D♭ G♭ C♭

F♯ Major (F♯ A♯ C♯)
SYMBOL (F♯) 6 sharps
F♯ C♯ G♯ D♯ A♯ E♯

G♭ Major and F♯ Major are the same chord. G♭ IS F♯. As previously mentioned, all of the patterns are moveable, since no open strings are used.
To play the G♭ or F♯ major chords, lower all of the G major patterns one fret. Transposition is fairly simple if one understands the process.

12

A Major (A C♯ E) 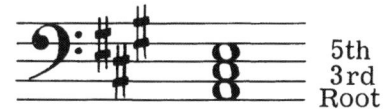 SYMBOL (A)

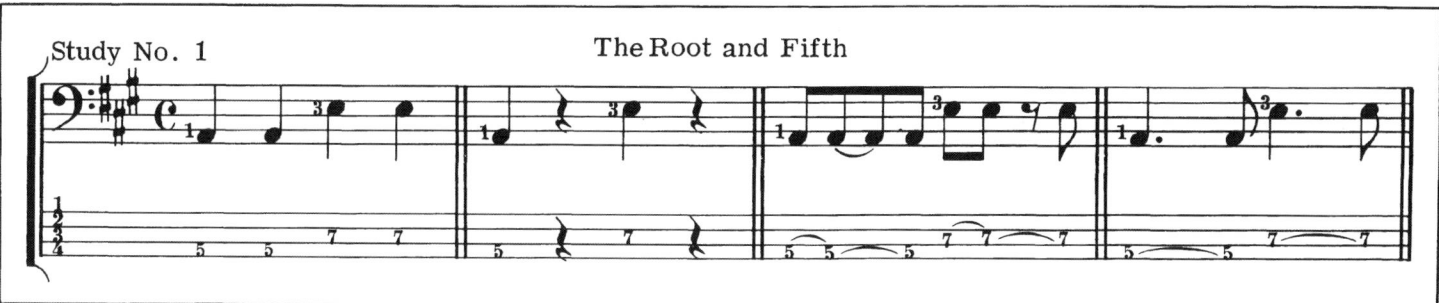

The easiest pattern to transpose is that which begins with the root on the 4th string. Begin any of the A Major patterns (starting on the 4th string) and lower one fret, to the 4th fret and you will produce the A♭ Major chord. Begin this same pattern at the 6th fret and you will play the B♭ Major chord. Play the same at the 7th fret and you will have the B Major chord. It's Fun! Try it.

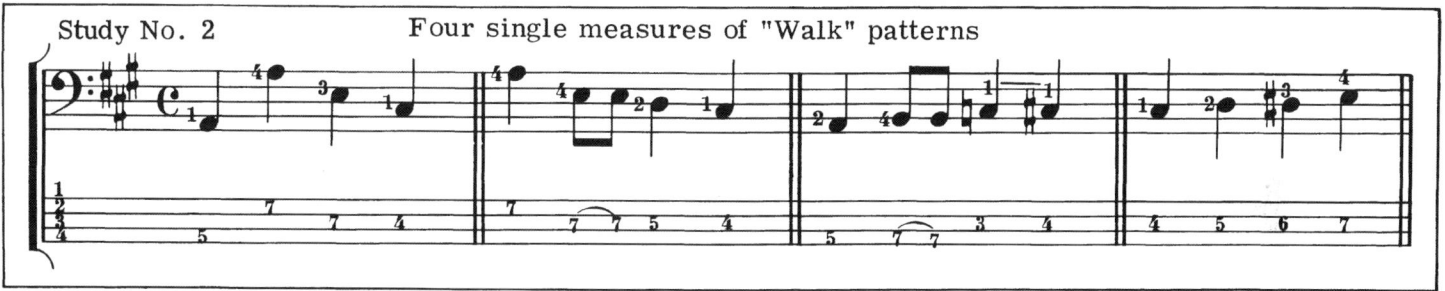

"Walk" and "Pop" patterns in studies #2 and #3 can be changed to A♭ major by lowering A major one fret.

Transposition chart for all A Major chord patterns beginning on 4th string

FRET	3	4	5	6	7	8	9	10	11	12
CHORD	G	A♭	A	B♭	B	C	D♭	D	E♭	E

A♭ Major (A♭ C E♭)
4 Flats
B♭ E♭ A♭ D♭

SYMBOL (A♭)

A♭ Major and G♯ Major are the same chord. All A Major patterns are moveable. Lower any of the studies 1 through 4 ONE fret and this will give you the A♭ Major Chord. Use notes or tablature.

| B♭ Major (B♭ D F) |

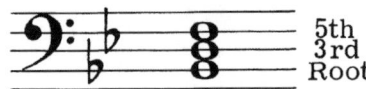 SYMBOL (B♭)

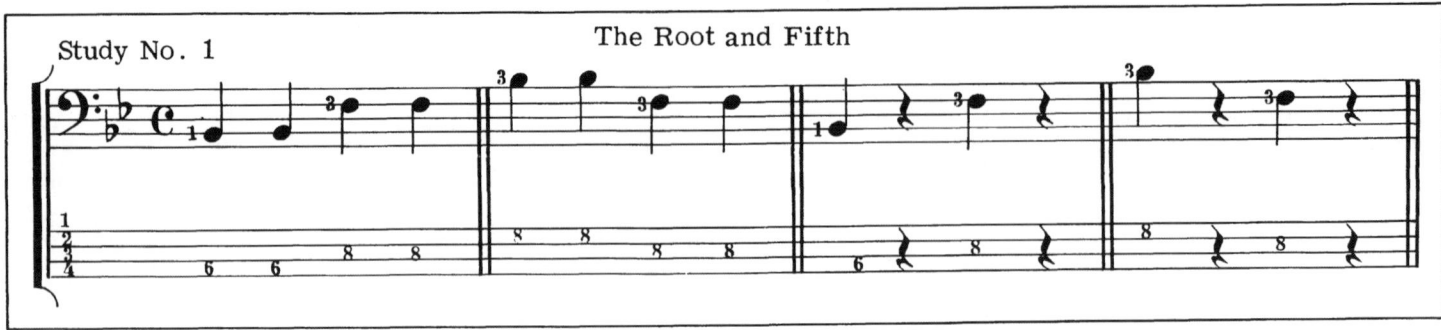

When studying spend your time wisely. Do NOT attempt to learn all of the patterns at one time. Memorize one or two at the most, learn to use these with good taste and when you are sure that you know these then you can add one pattern at a time. In the beginning, play the usual "Rock" or "Blues" tunes of twelve bars, using the tunes with three changes. When satisfied that you can perform these tunes well you may then expand to the tunes with more chords. Use good common sense. You can't miss.

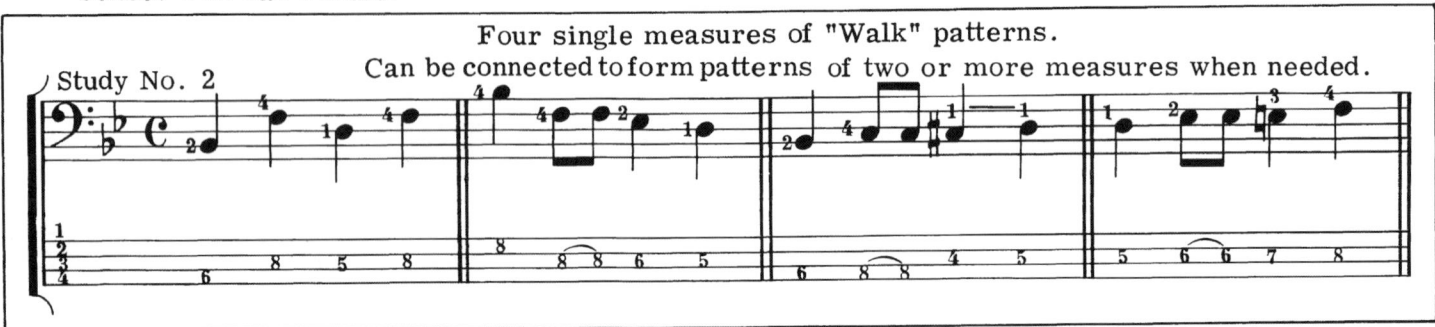

The three chord "Blues" twelve bar patterns are known in musical notation as the Tonic or 1st note of the scale. The Sub-Dominant, or 4th note of the scale and the Dominant Seventh which is the 5th note of the scale. Therefore, in B♭, the three principal chords will be the B♭ Major, the E♭ Major and the F7th chords.

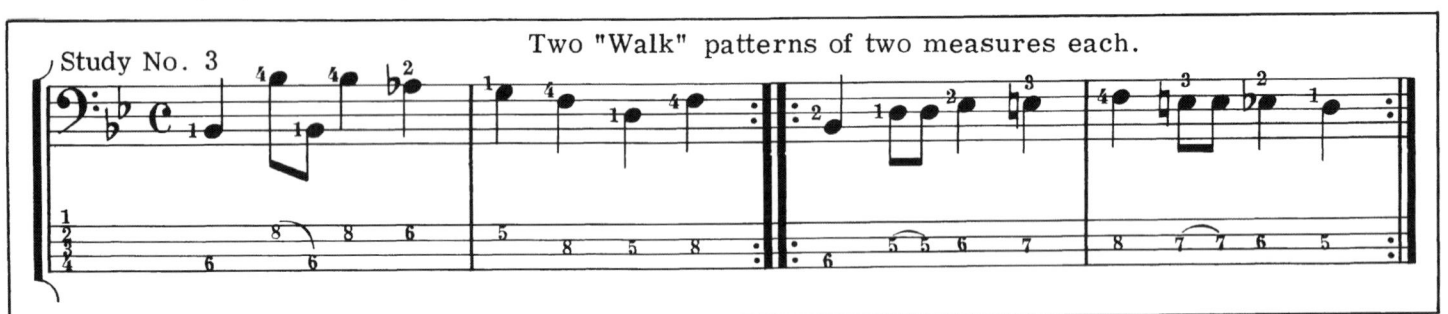

Study No. 4 — 3/4 time patterns. Raise the A Major patterns one fret higher.

 SYMBOL (B)

B Major and C♭ Major are the SAME. All of the B♭ patterns are moveable. Raise any of the studies No. 1 through No. 4 and this will give you the B Major or C♭ Major Chords. Use notes or tablature.

Example below.

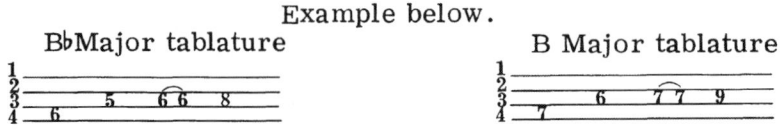

C Minor
C E♭ G

5th
3rd
Root

SYMBOL (Cm)

Study No. 1

The Root and Fifth
The Root and Fifth pattern is the same for the C minor
chord as it is for the C Major chord.

Four single measures of "Walk" patterns

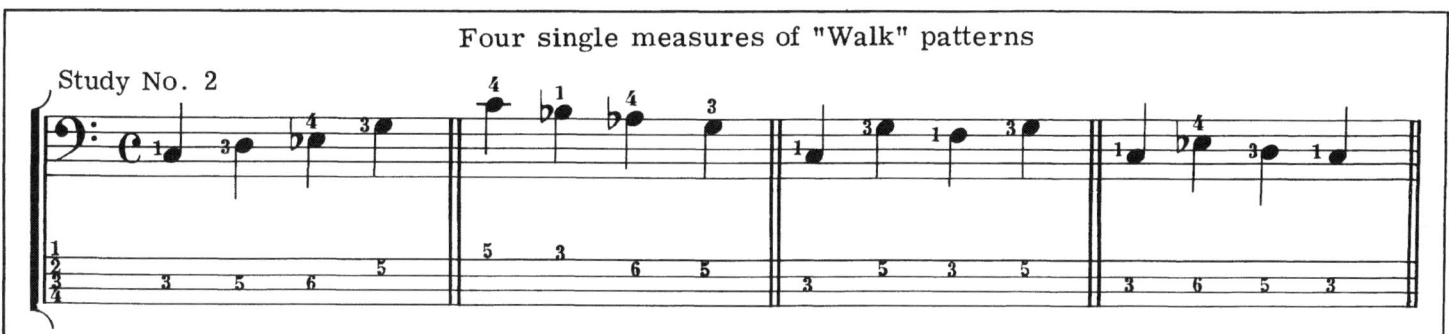

Study No. 2 is played in 3rd position. Try it in 8th position. Use same fingering, add five frets to the tablature, then LOWER each note one string. See the example below.

EXAMPLE

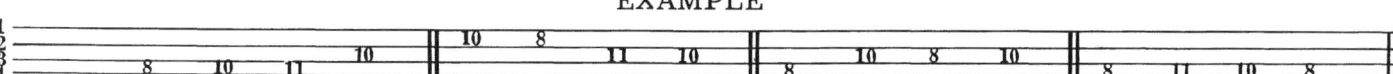

Two "Walk" patterns of two measures each.

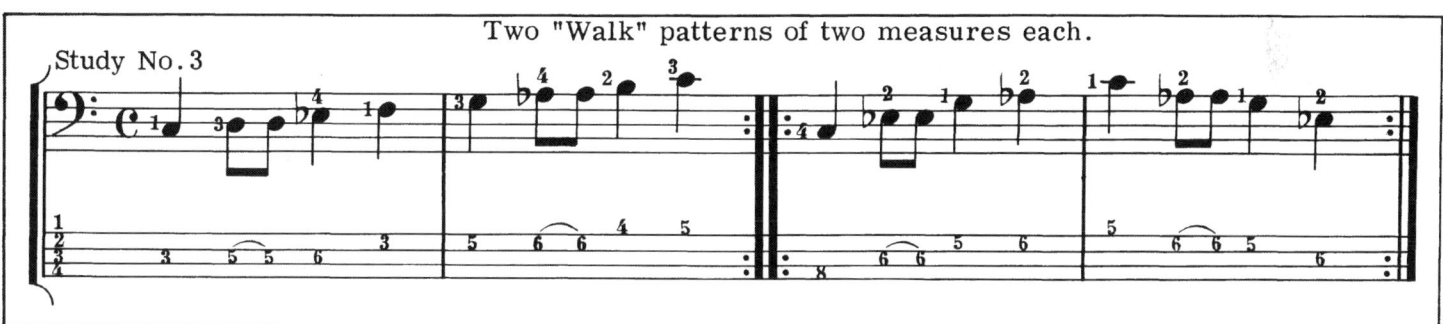

Play with a well defined solid beat in "Walk" style. Just a reminder
that all suggested fingering is optional. If you can come up with a better
fingering... USE IT! YOU are the BASSIST.

3/4 time patterns

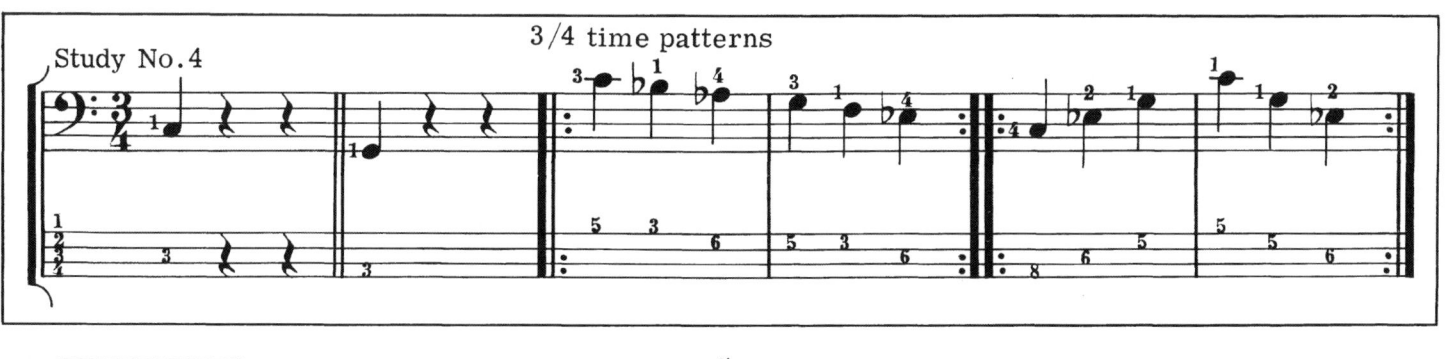

C♯ minor
C♯ E G♯

5th
3rd
Root

SYMBOL (C♯m)

All of the C minor patterns are moveable. To play a C♯ minor chord use any
of the C minor patterns, refer to the tablature and RAISE each note one fret.

EXAMPLE

15

D Minor (D F A)  SYMBOL (D m)

Study No. 1

The Root and Fifth
The Root and Fifth pattern is the same for the
D Minor chord as it is for the D Major chord.

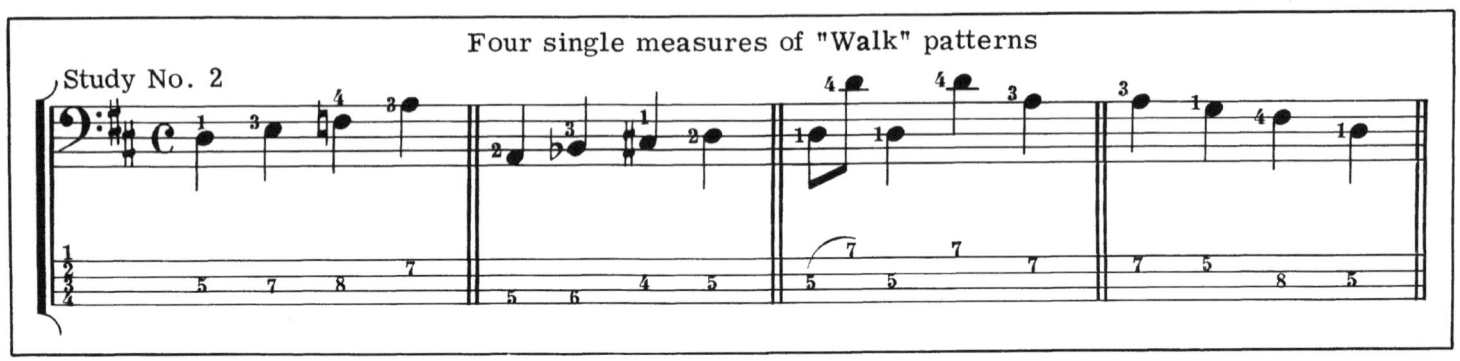

For variety the rhythmic figures below can be applied to any "Walk" pattern. Wherever there is a "Walk" of four beats to the measure, the substitution of <u>two</u> eighth notes for ANY quarter note gives you the necessary change in rhythm to create the "professional sound". See example below.

Db Minor (Db Fb Ab)   SYMBOL (Db m)

All of the D Minor patterns are moveable. To play the Db minor chord you can use any of the D minor patterns, refer to the tablature and <u>lower</u> each note one fret.

EXAMPLE

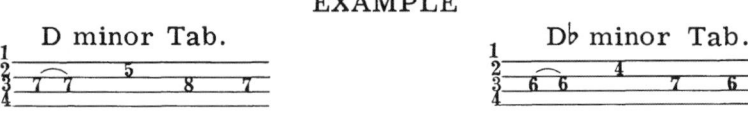

16

E Minor (E G B)		SYMBOL (Em)

Study No. 1	The Root and Fifth The Root and Fifth pattern is the same for the E Minor chord as it is for the E Major chord.

Four single measures of "Walk" patterns

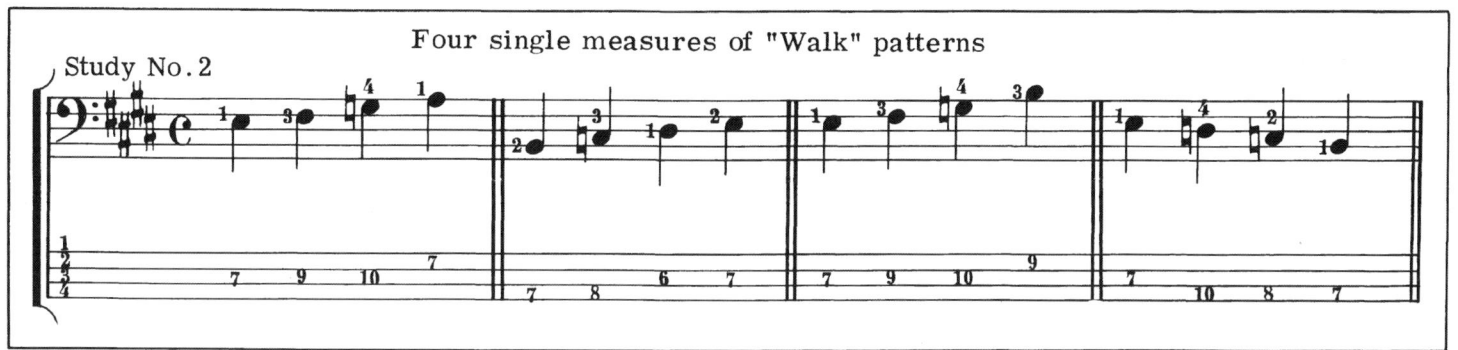

Two "Walk" patterns of two measures each.
Play with "solid" beat.

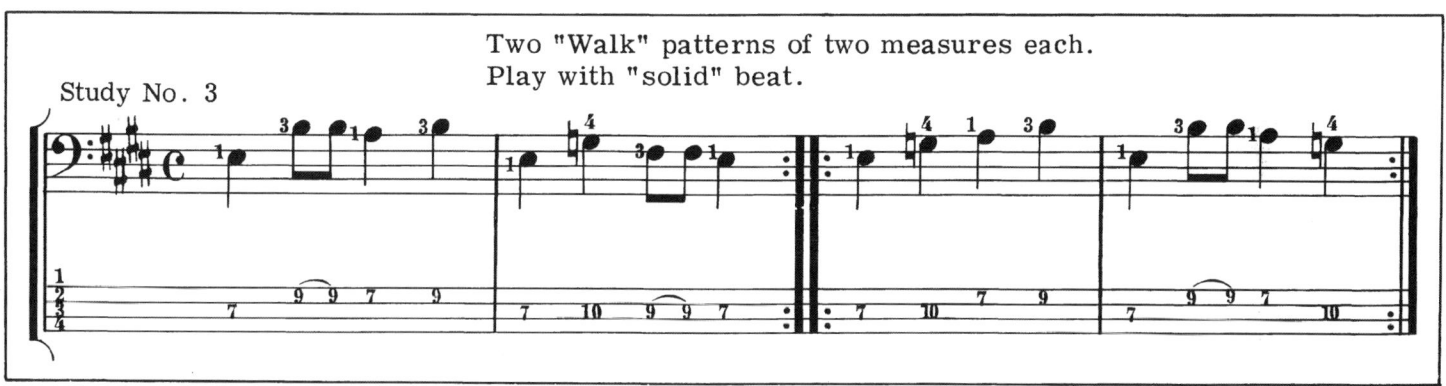

To get that "Real" solid "Walk" beat and feeling we suggest that you play eighth notes as if they are quasi dotted eighths and sixteenths.
Example:

Various 3/4 time patterns.

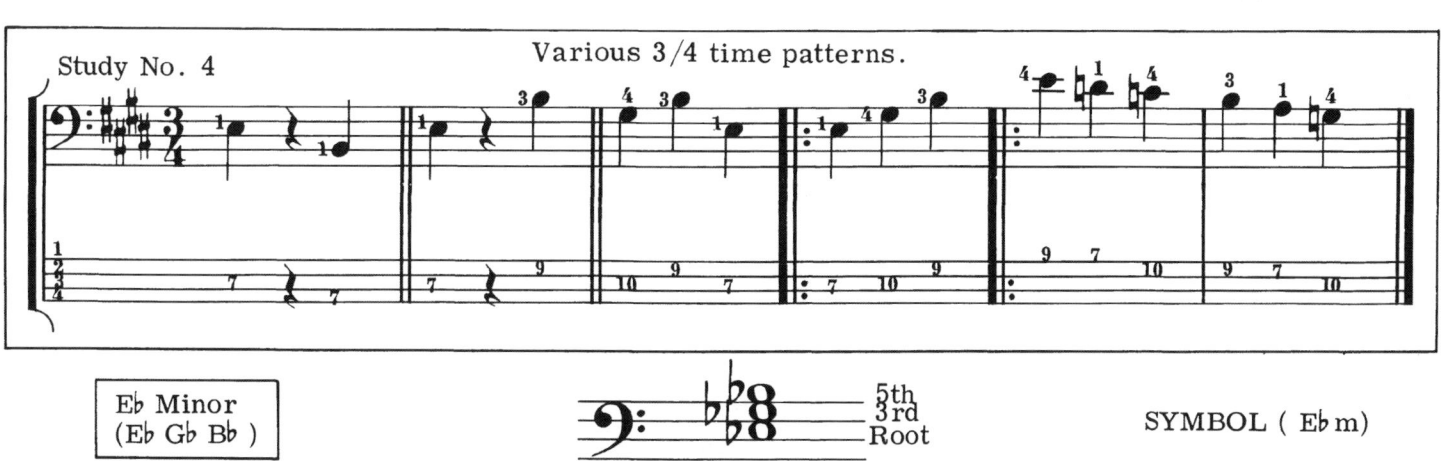

E♭ Minor (E♭ G♭ B♭)		SYMBOL (E♭m)

All of the E minor patterns are moveable. To play the E♭ minor chord you can use any of the E minor patterns, refer to the tablature and LOWER each note ONE fret.

EXAMPLE

17

F Minor
F A♭ C

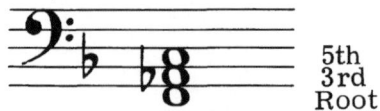

5th
3rd
Root

SYMBOL (Fm)

Study No. 1

The Root and Fifth
The Root and Fifth pattern is the same for the F minor chord as it is for the F major chord.

Study No. 2

Four single measures of "Walk" patterns

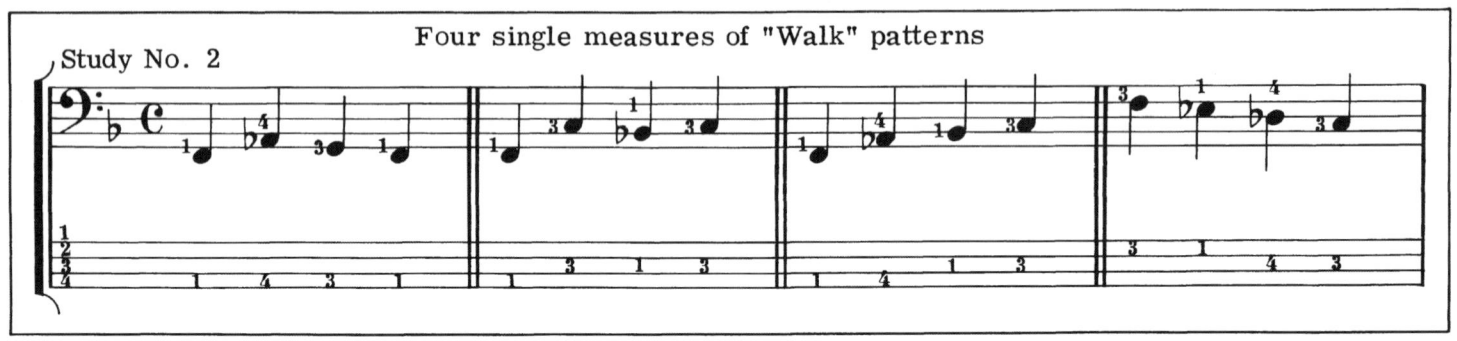

Study No. 3

Playing the same two measure pattern in two different positions.

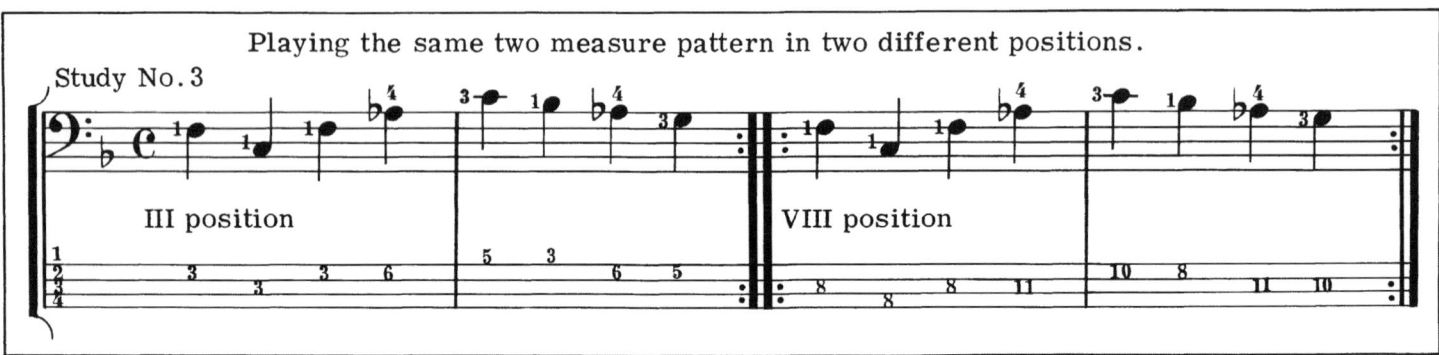

III position   VIII position

Any study that is played on the 1st, 2nd and 3rd strings can be played on the 2nd, 3rd and 4th strings by playing the pattern 5 frets HIGHER. You can learn a lot by experimenting. The notes are the SAME...fingering is the SAME.. only the tab and position are different.

Study No. 4

3/4 time study.
The Root and Fifth is same as in F Major

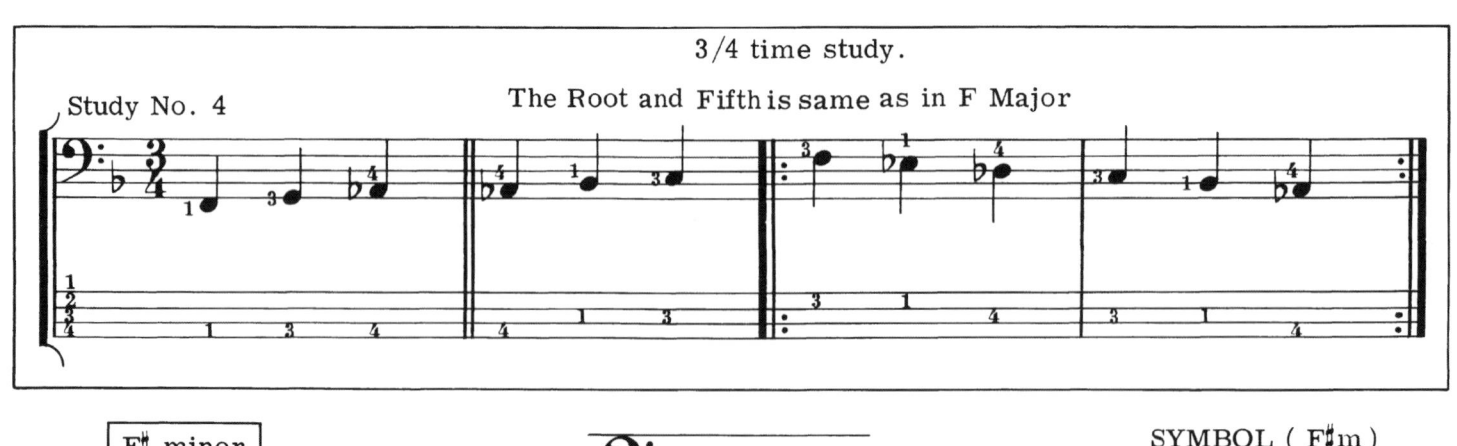

F♯ minor
F♯ A C♯

5th
3rd
Root

SYMBOL (F♯m)

All of the F minor patterns are moveable. To play the F♯ minor chord, take any of the F minor patterns, refer to the tab and RAISE each note ONE fret.

EXAMPLE

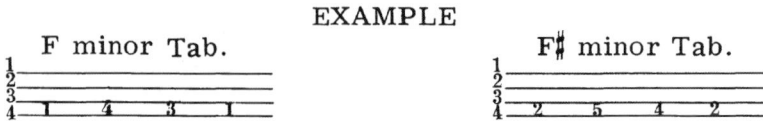

F minor Tab.   F♯ minor Tab.

| G Minor |
| G B♭ D |

SYMBOL (Gm)

Study No. 1
The Root and Fifth
The Root and Fifth pattern is the same for the G minor chord as it is for the G major chord.

Study No. 2 — Four single measures of "Walk" patterns.

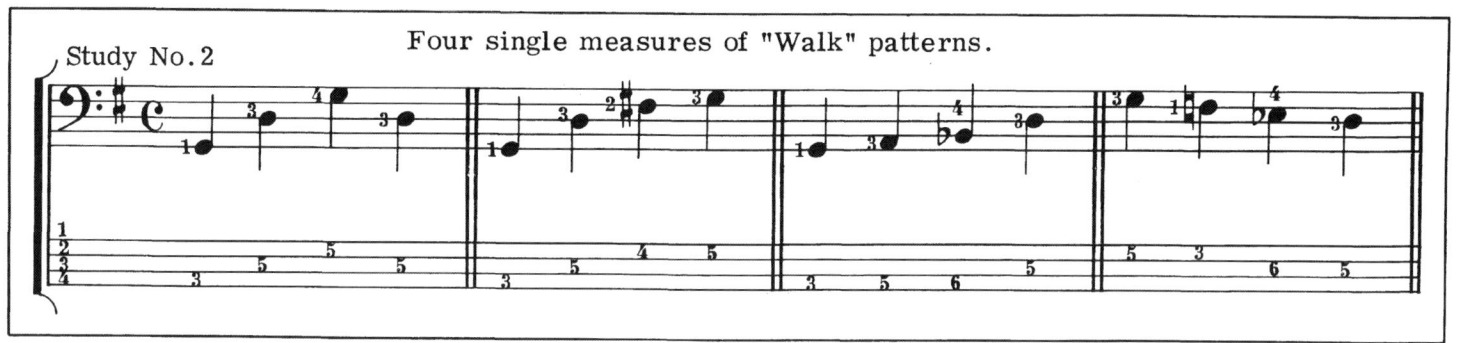

Study No. 3 — Two "Walk" patterns of two measures each.

Reminder: All suggested fingering is optional. Use your ideas on fingering if you think you can improve what is suggested. You can also change positions where possible and practical. See the F Minor page foot-note in study No. 3 for explantion.

Study No. 4 — An assortment of 3/4 time patterns.

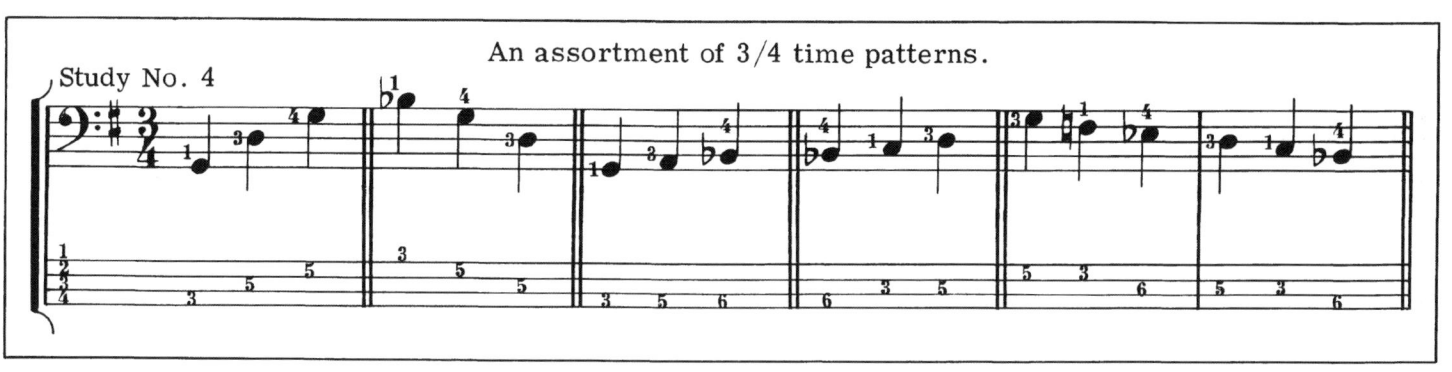

| G♯ Minor |
| G♯ B D♯ |

SYMBOL (G♯m)

All of the G minor patterns are moveable. To play the G♯ minor chord, take any of the G minor patterns, refer to the tab and RAISE each note ONE fret.

EXAMPLE

A Minor A C E	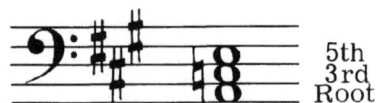 5th 3rd Root	SYMBOL (Am)

Study No. 1 — The Root and Fifth
The Root and Fifth pattern is the same for the A minor chord as it is for the A Major chord.

Study No. 2 — Four single measures of "Walk" patterns.

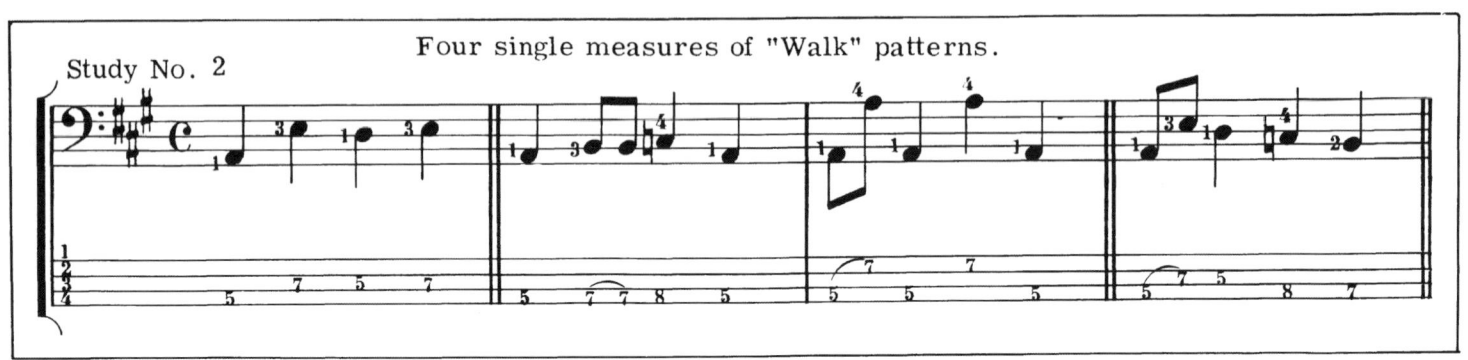

Study No. 3 — Two "Walk" patterns of two measures each.

All suggested fingering is optional. You may also change rhythmic figures wherever you wish. See foot-note example, the D minor page study No. 3

Study No. 4 — Four single measure studies in 3/4 time.

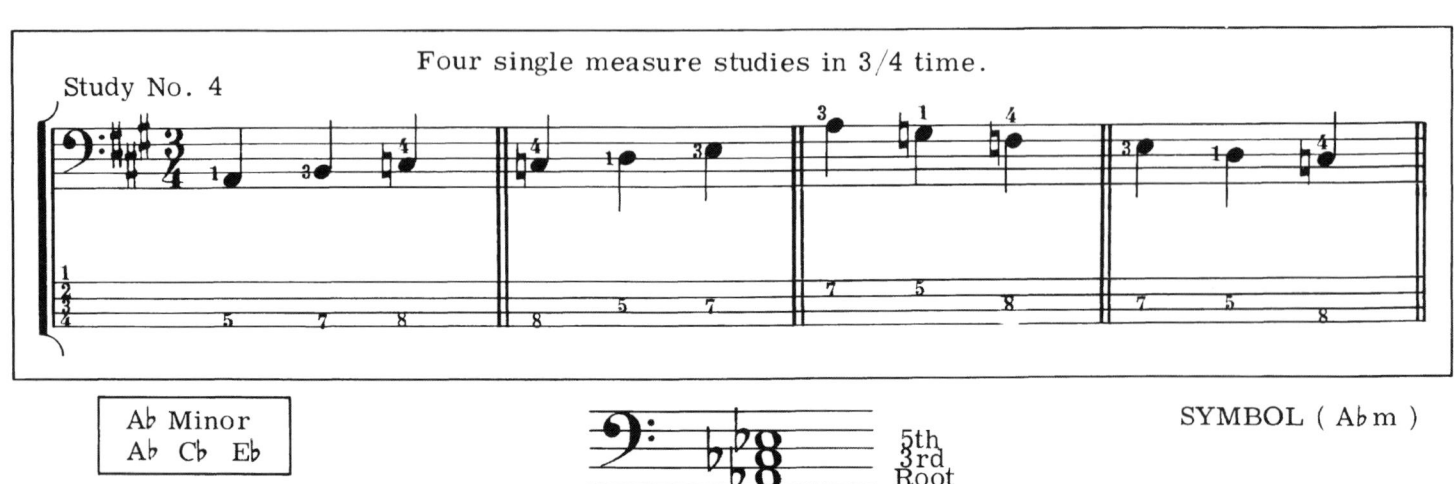

A♭ Minor A♭ C♭ E♭	5th 3rd Root	SYMBOL (A♭m)

All of the A minor patterns are moveable. To play the A♭ minor chord, take any of the A minor patterns, refer to the tab and **LOWER** each note ONE fret.

EXAMPLE

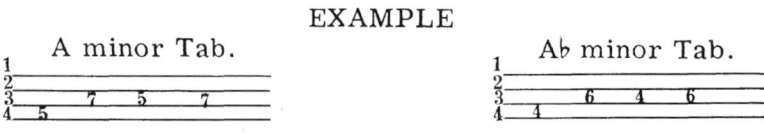

20

B Minor
B D F♯

SYMBOL (Bm)

Study No. 1 — The Root and Fifth
The Root and Fifth is the same for the B Minor chord as it is for the B Major chord.

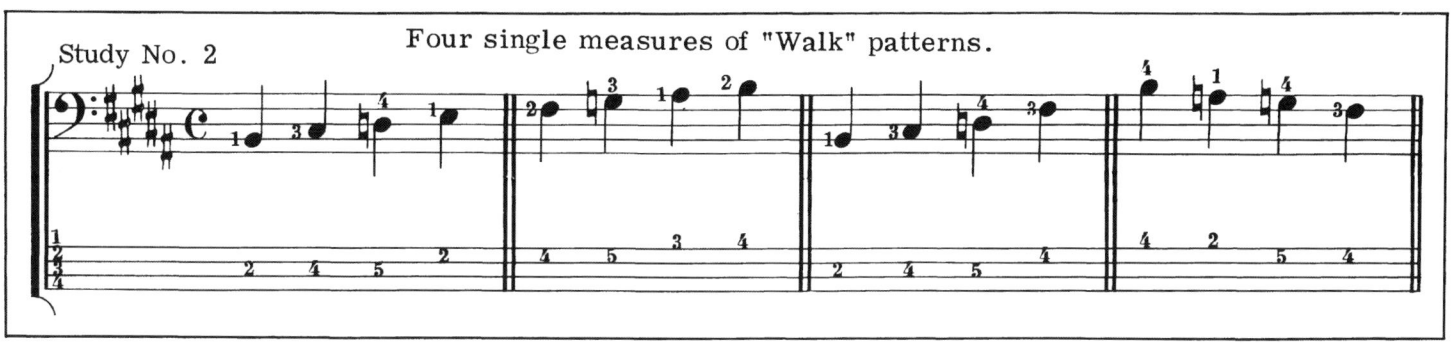

Study No. 2 — Four single measures of "Walk" patterns.

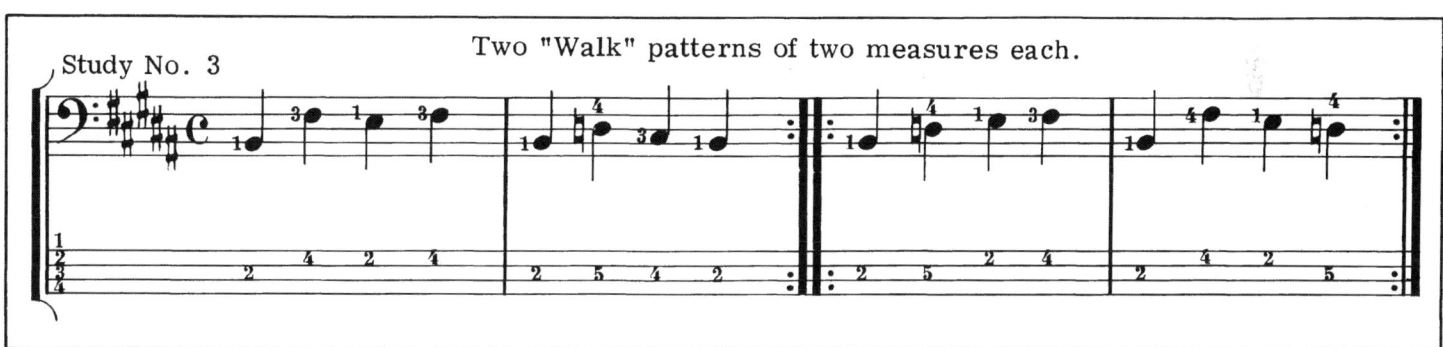

Study No. 3 — Two "Walk" patterns of two measures each.

Study No. 4 — 3/4 time studies

B♭ Minor
B♭ D♭ F

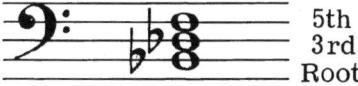

SYMBOL (B♭m)

All of the B Minor patterns are moveable. To play the B♭ minor chord, take any of the B Minor patterns, refer to the Tab and LOWER each note one fret.

EXAMPLE

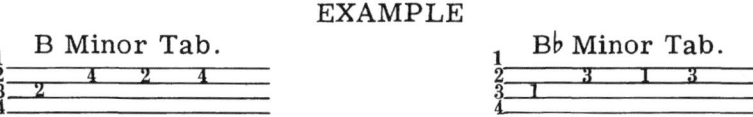

C Seventh
C E G B♭

SYMBOL (C7)

Study No. 1	The Root and Fifth The Root and Fifth pattern is the same for the C Seventh chord as it is for the C Major chord.

Study No. 2 — Four single measures in "Walk" style

Study No. 3 — Two "Walk" patterns of two measures each

All of the chord studies No. 2 and No. 3 are played on the 1st, 2nd and 3rd strings. You can change the position of these chord studies by playing them on the 2nd, 3rd and 4th strings, using the same fingering and playing each pattern five (5) frets HIGHER. The mechanics of changing positions can be applied to any study where the possibility exists.

Study No. 4	3/4 time patterns. For all C7th chords in 3/4 time use any of the C Major patterns in Study No. 4

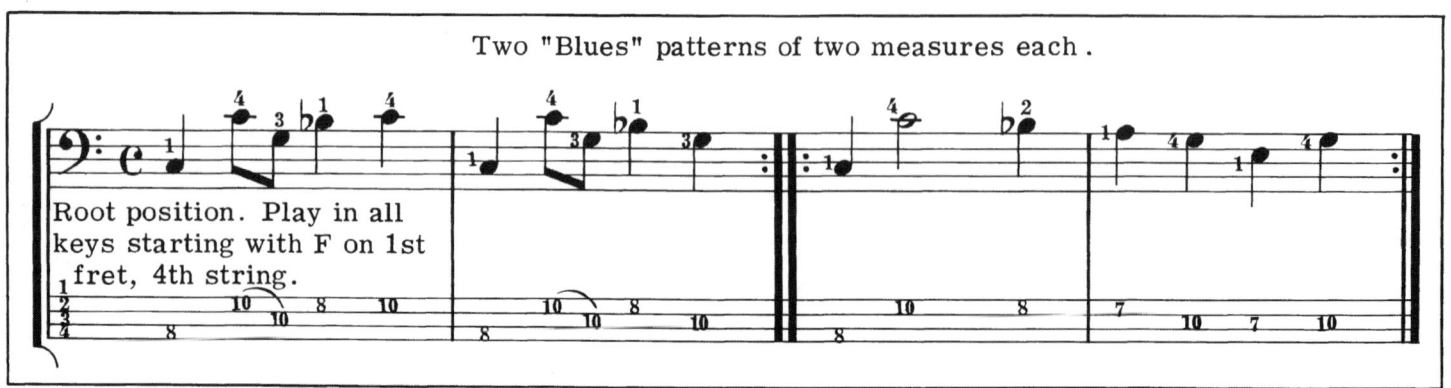

Two "Blues" patterns of two measures each.

Root position. Play in all keys starting with F on 1st fret, 4th string.

D Seventh
D F# A C

SYMBOL (D7)

Study No. 1 — The Root and Fifth
The Root and Fifth pattern is the same for the D7 chord as it is for the D Major Chord.

Single measure patterns: "Walk" style

Study No. 2

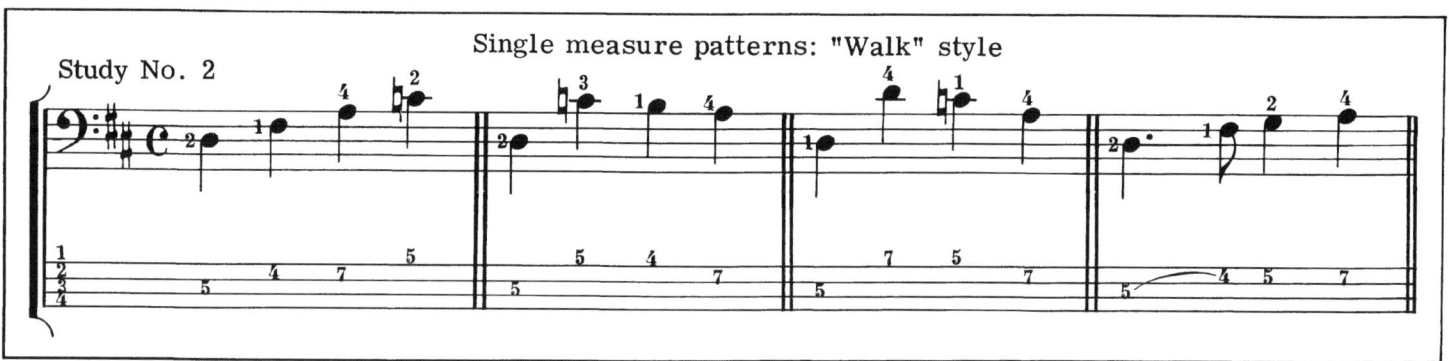

The above studies are all in "root" patterns: meaning that each individual measure begins with the root. All are written on the 1st, 2nd and 3rd strings. Move these studies to the 2nd, 3rd and 4th strings, then add five frets to the tablature and you will have the same chord pattern with the same fingering, same tones, only higher on the neck.

Study No. 3 — Two "Walk" patterns of two measures each.

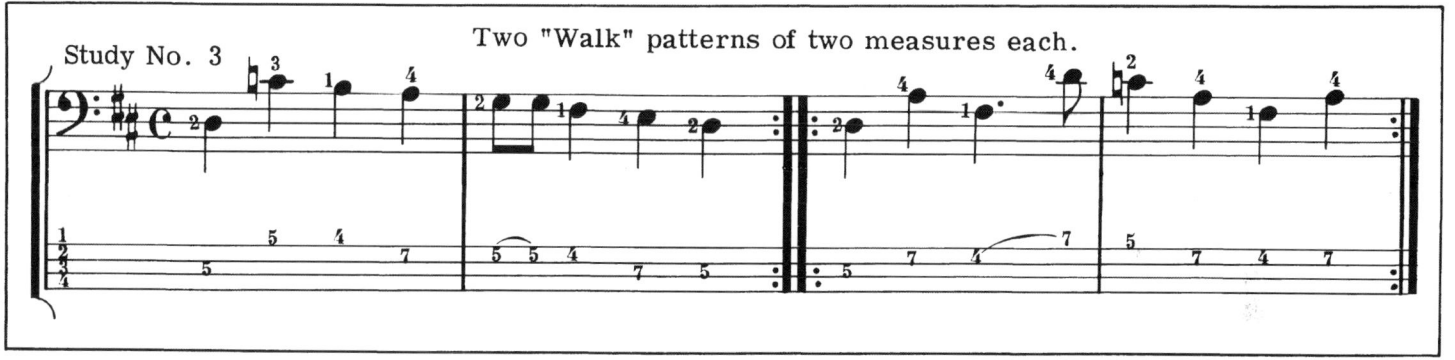

3/4 time patterns.

Study No. 4

For all D7th chords in 3/4 time use any of the D Major patterns in study No. 4

SYMBOL (Db7)

Db7 and C#7 are the same chord. Since all of the D7th patterns are moveable, (no open strings) you can use any of the above D7th patterns, refer to the tablature and **LOWER** each note **ONE** fret. This will give you the Db7 chord.

EXAMPLE

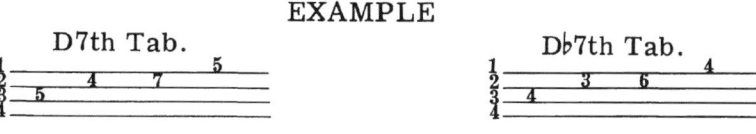

23

E Seventh
E G# B D

SYMBOL (E7)

Study No. 1	The Root and Fifth The Root and Fifth pattern is the same for the E7 chord as it is for the E Major chord.

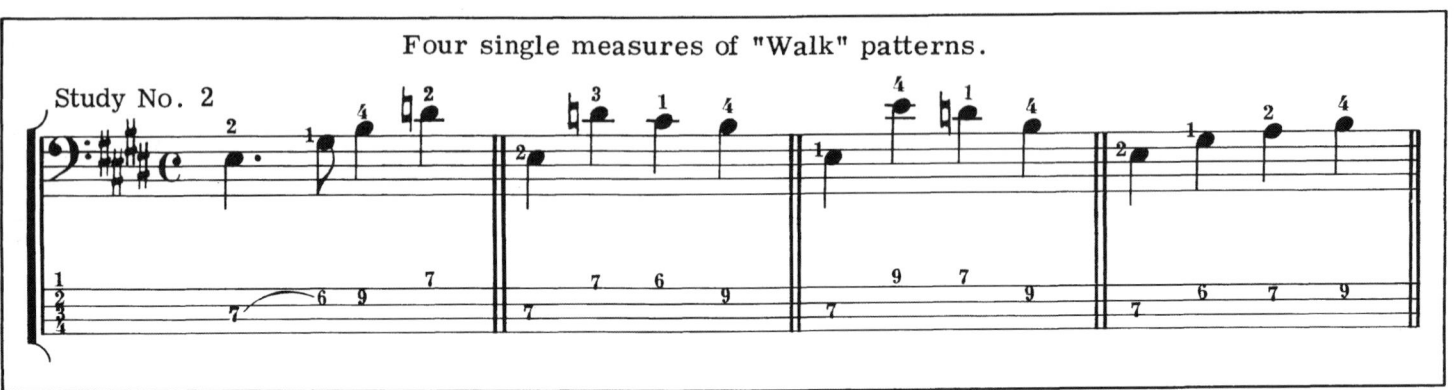

TO IMPROVE YOUR KNOWLEDGE OF POSITIONS SEE THE MEL BAY
PUBLICATION "ELECTRIC BASS POSITION STUDIES."

Study No. 4	3/4 time patterns. For all E7th chords in 3/4 time use any of the E Major patterns in study No. 4

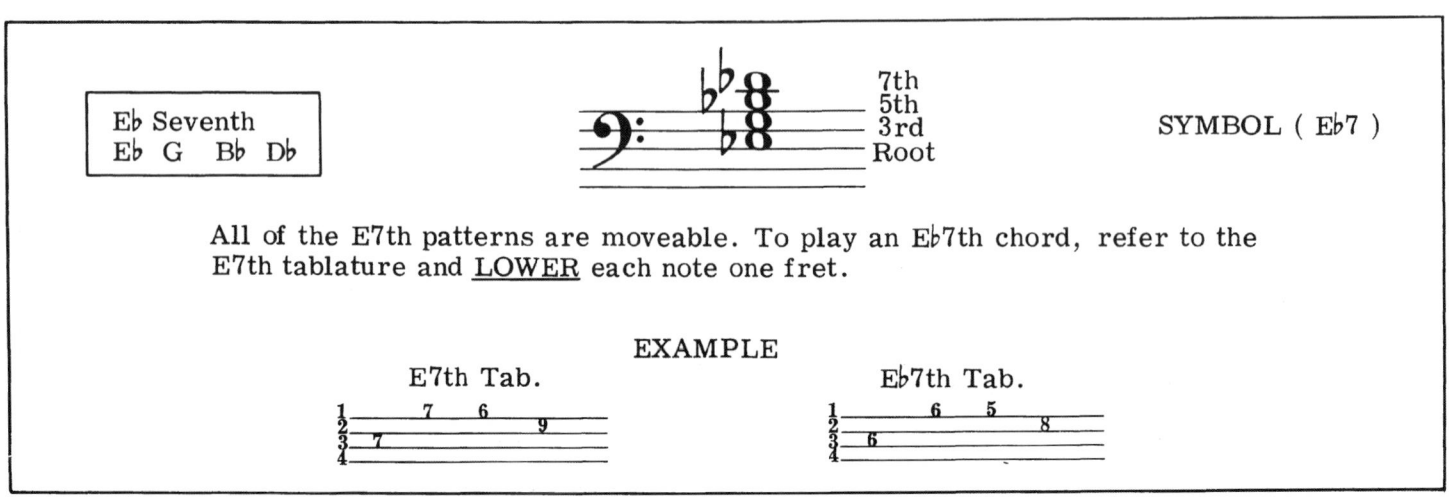

24

F Seventh
F A C E♭

SYMBOL (F7)

Study No. 1	The Root and Fifth The Root and Fifth pattern is the same for the F7th chord as it is for the F Major chord.

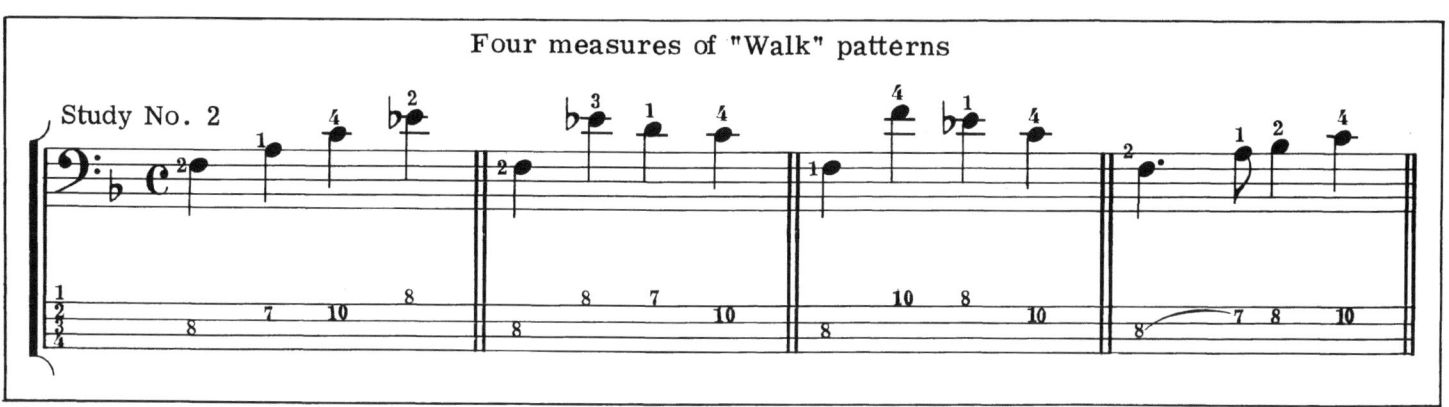

Study No. 2 — Four measures of "Walk" patterns

Study No. 3 — Two "Walk" patterns of two measures each.

Study No. 4	3/4 time patterns For all F7th chords in 3/4 time use any of the F Major patterns in study No. 4

F# Seventh
F# A# C# E

SYMBOL (F#7)

All F7th chord patterns are moveable. To play the F#7th chord, refer to the F7th tablature and <u>RAISE</u> each note <u>ONE</u> fret.

EXAMPLE

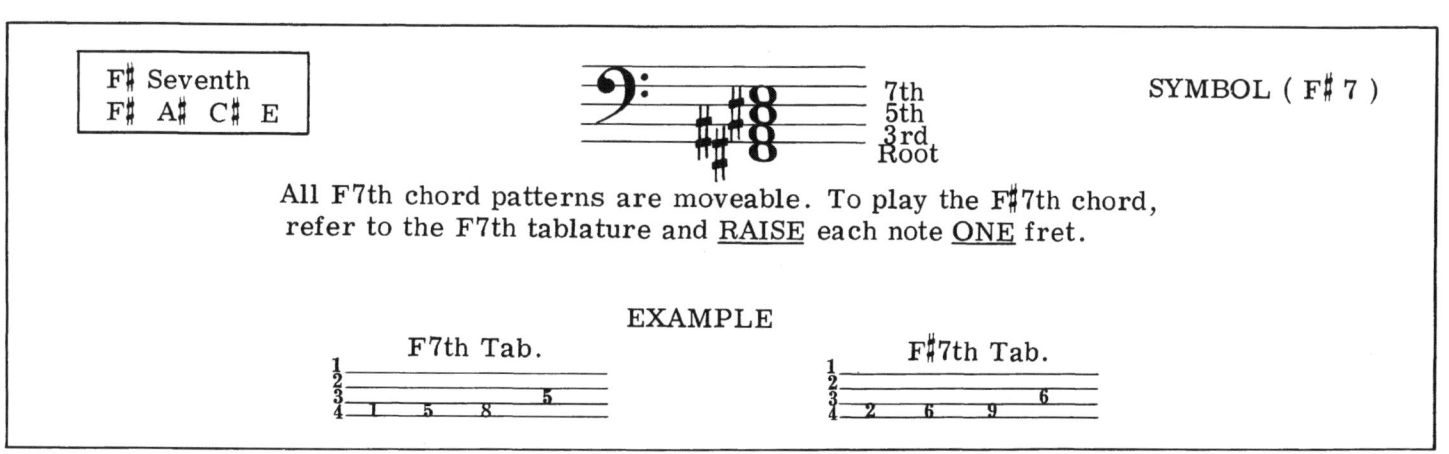

25

G Seventh
G B D F

SYMBOL (G7)

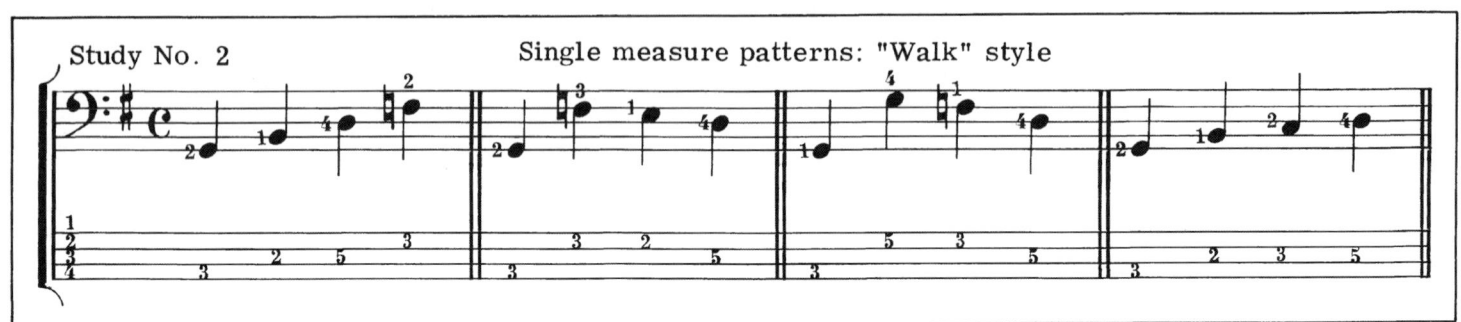

Study No. 1	The Root and Fifth
	The Root and Fifth pattern is the same for the G7th chord as it is for the G Major chord.

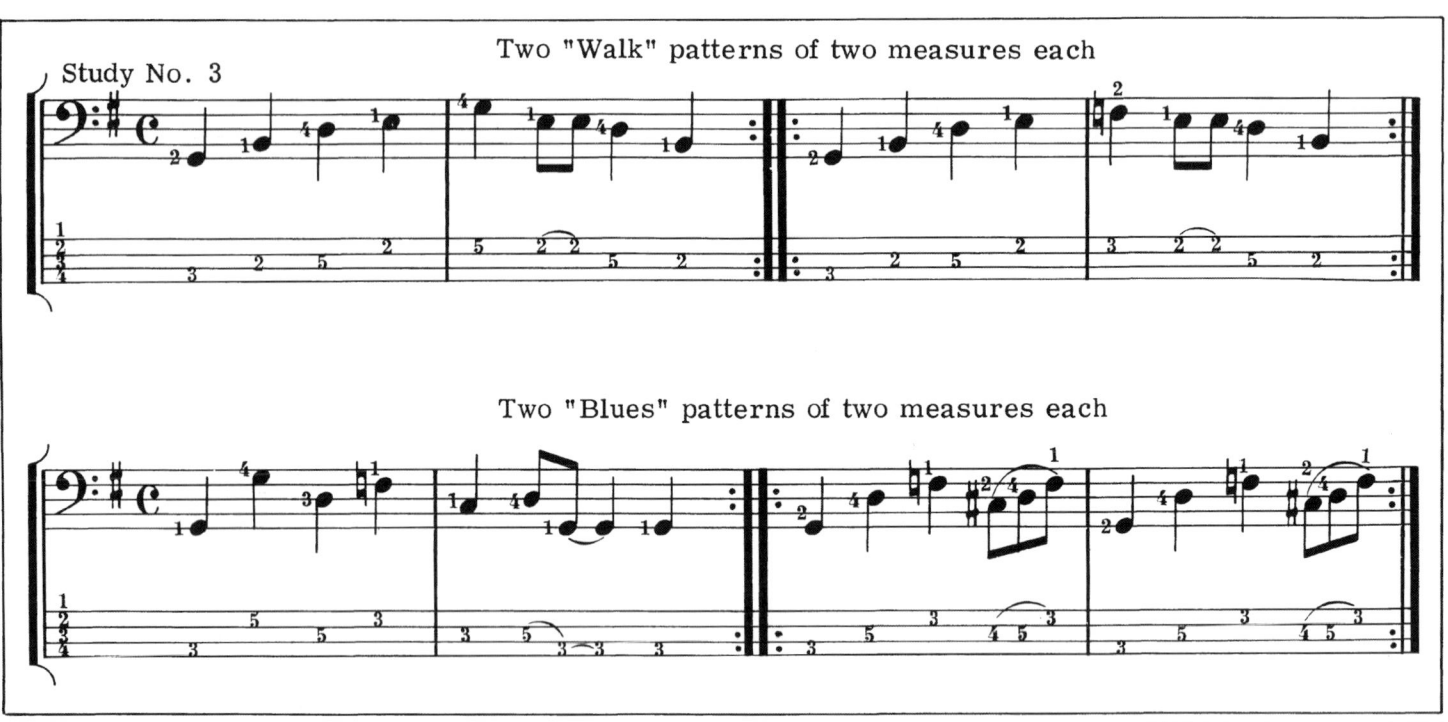

Study No. 2 — Single measure patterns: "Walk" style

Study No. 3 — Two "Walk" patterns of two measures each

Two "Blues" patterns of two measures each

Study No. 4	3/4 time patterns
	For all G7th chords in 3/4 time use any of the G Major patterns in study No. 4

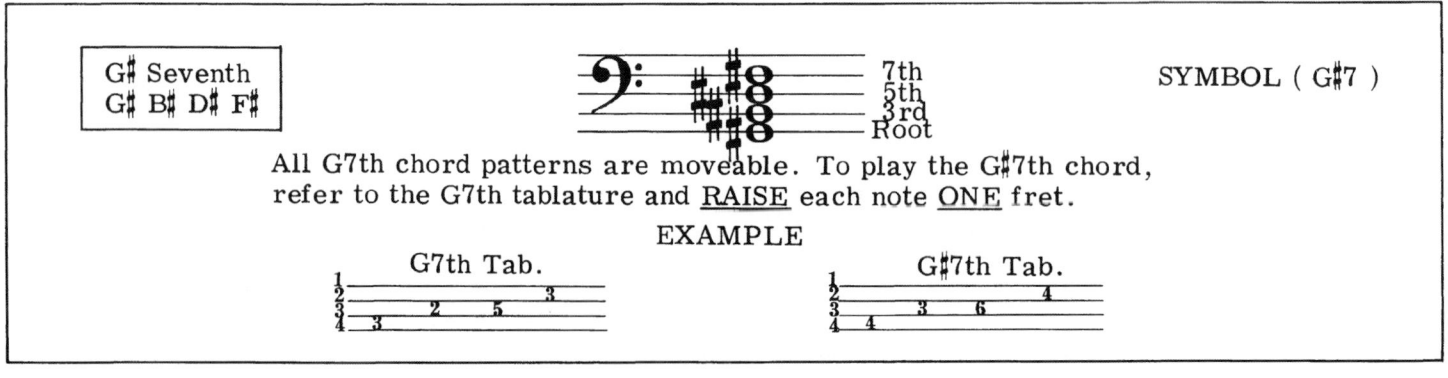

G# Seventh
G# B# D# F#

SYMBOL (G#7)

All G7th chord patterns are moveable. To play the G#7th chord, refer to the G7th tablature and RAISE each note ONE fret.

EXAMPLE

26

A Seventh
A C# E G

SYMBOL (A7)

Study No. 1 — The Root and Fifth
The Root and Fifth pattern is the same for the A7th chord as it is for the A Major chord.

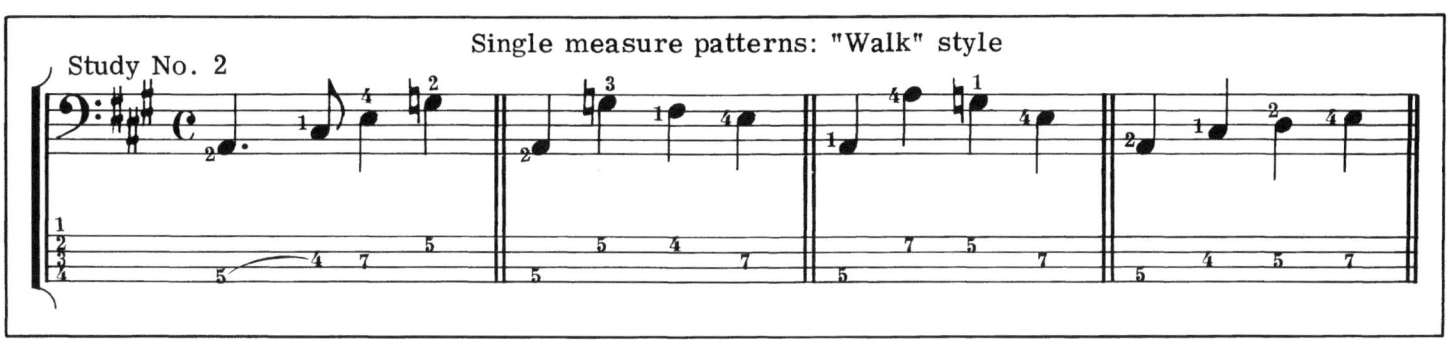

Study No. 2 — Single measure patterns: "Walk" style

Study No. 3 — Two "Walk" patterns of two measures each

Two "Blues" patterns of two measures each

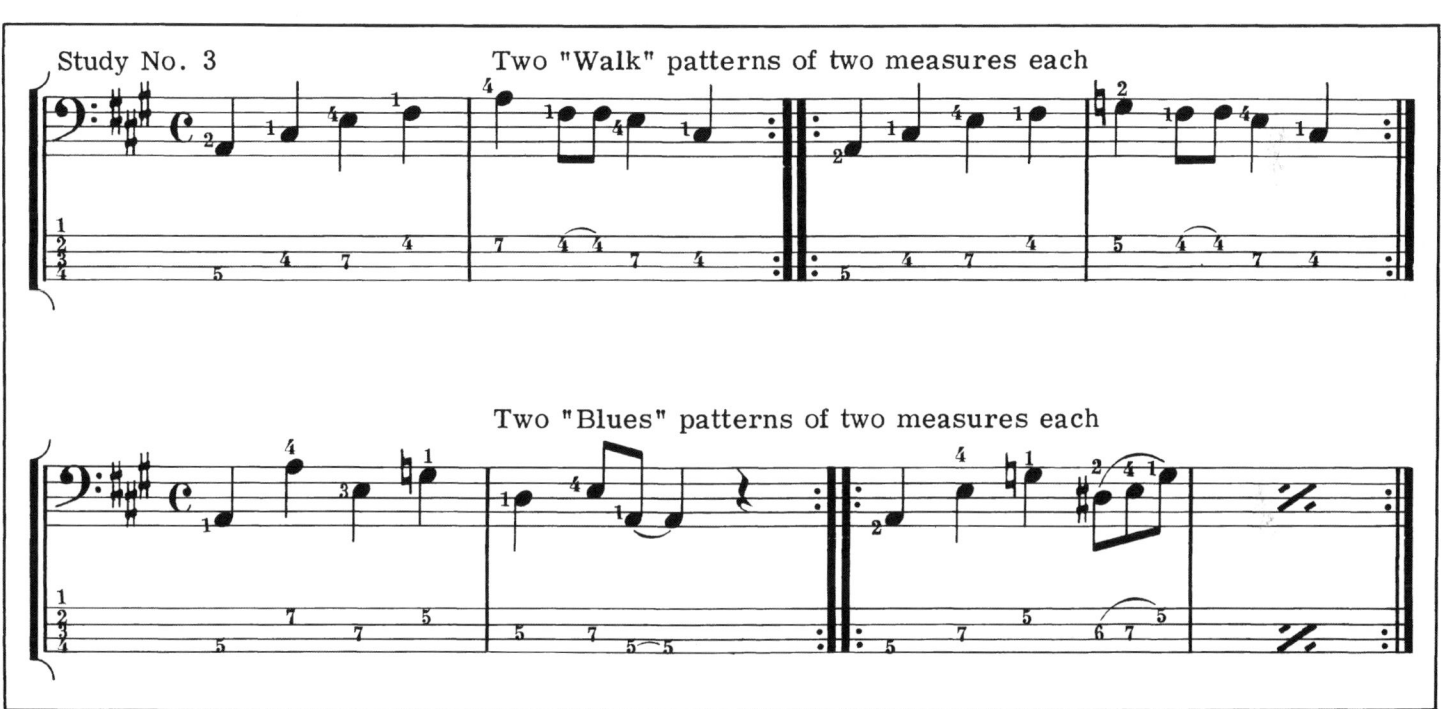

Study No. 4 — 3/4 time patterns
For all A7th chords in 3/4 time use any of the A Major patterns in study No. 4

Ab Seventh
Ab C Eb Gb

SYMBOL (Ab7)

All A7th chord patterns are moveable. To play the Ab7th chord refer to the A7th tablature and LOWER each note ONE fret.

EXAMPLE

B Seventh
B D# F# A

SYMBOL (B7)

Study No. 1 — The Root and Fifth
The Root and Fifth pattern is the same for the B7th chord as it is for the B Major chord.

Study No. 2 — Single measure patterns: "Walk" style

Study No. 3 — Two "Walk" patterns of two measures each

Two "Rock" "Blues" patterns of two measures each

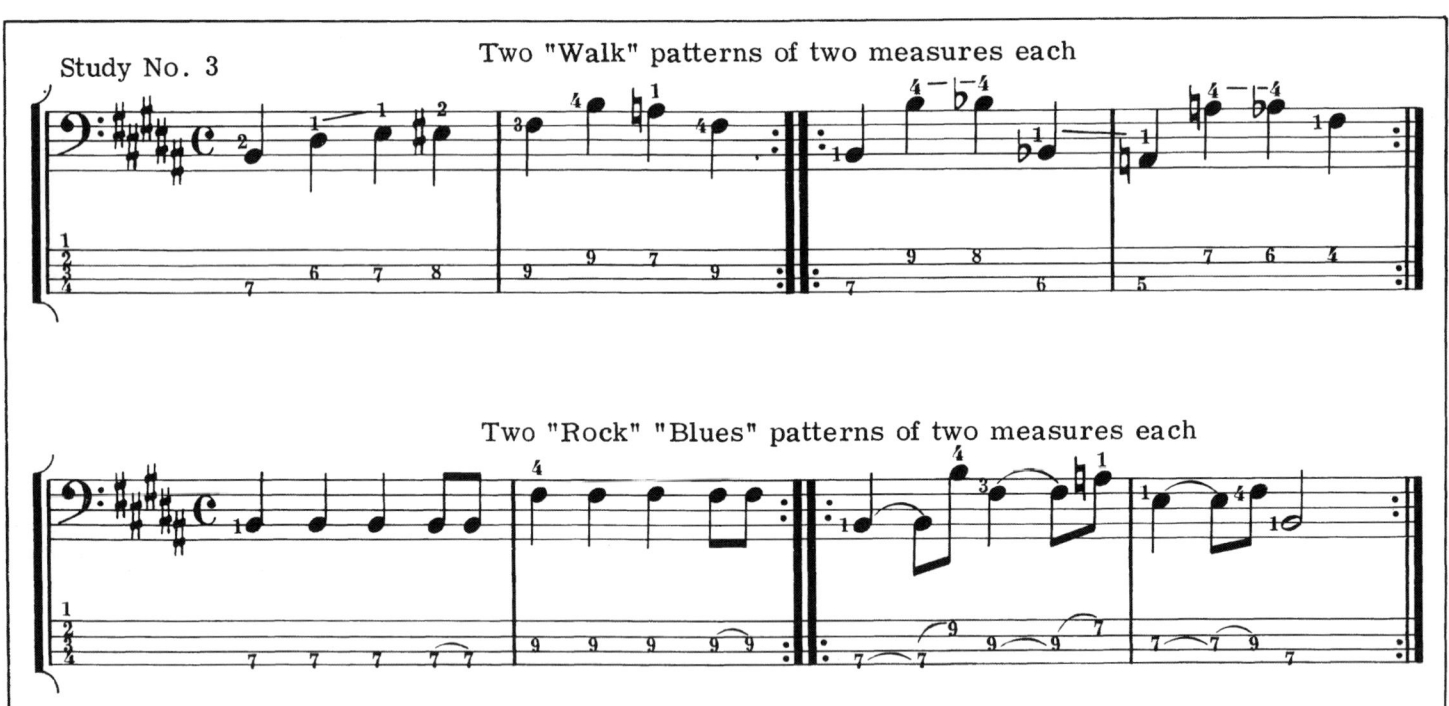

Study No. 4 — 3/4 time patterns
For all B7th chords in 3/4 time use any of the B Major patterns in study No. 4

Bb Seventh
Bb D F Ab

SYMBOL (Bb7)

All B7th chord patterns are moveable. To play the Bb7th chord refer to the B7 tablature and LOWER each note ONE fret.

EXAMPLE

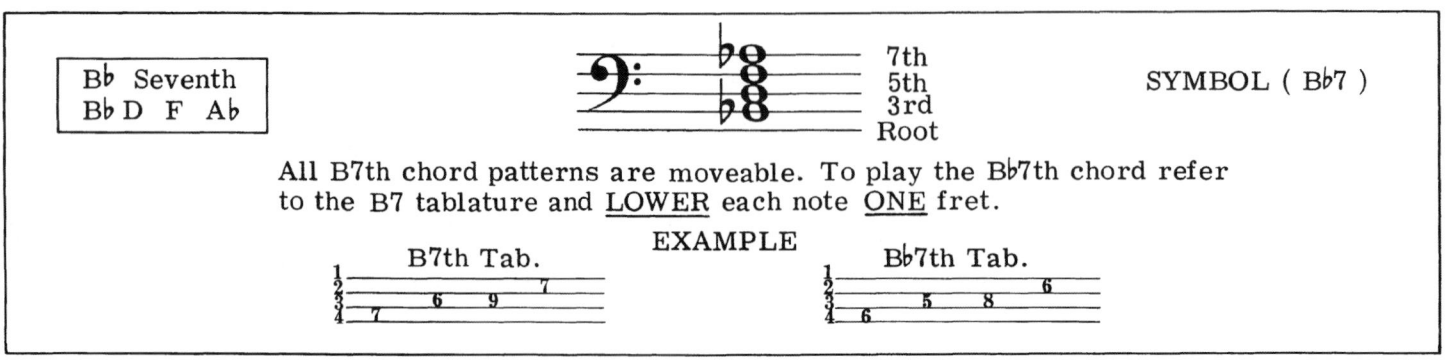

28

Printed in Great Britain
by Amazon